KILTY AS HELL

KILTY SERIES: BOOK SIX

Amy Vansant

CHAPTER ONE

Fiona entered her apartment building's private garage.

That's when she saw the boy.

She had no idea how old he was. She wasn't good at guessing kids' ages. He was small, so... Two? Six? Eight?

Who knows?

His age wasn't important. The important part was that the little brat was sitting on the hood of her car.

"Hey!" she snapped, speeding her step. "Get *off* of there."

"Watch your tone, young lady," said the boy.

Fiona stopped.

Oh no.

A seed of dread grew in the pit of her stomach.

It can't be.

She took a few steps forward, squinting at the boy in the dim light of the garage. He stared back at her with icy blue eyes.

Shit.

"Dad?" she asked.

The boy scoffed. "Yes. Of course, it's me. Who else would it be?"

His cadence mimicked that of her ever-irritable father, Rune, but his tone had a higher pitch—as if someone had sped Rune's voice like a chipmunk's.

She motioned to him as if she were lassoing him with her index finger.

"Is it me? I remember you taller."

The boy scowled. "I had to start over, and I miscalculated the year. I wanted to return to *this* year as an adult but...I was reborn six years ago instead of twenty."

He sighed.

Fiona noticed something. The last time she'd seen her father, he had one metal arm. He'd lost the original to her sister Catriona's adoptive father, Sean, in some modern-day sword fight.

How he managed to get himself roped into that...

She didn't care. To say Catriona and she had a complicated relationship with their father was like saying police had a *complicated* relationship with serial killers. To be fair, *complicated* was the only relationship anyone *could* have with Rune.

"You got your arm back," she said.

He glanced at his little hand.

"Yes. Look, I don't have much time—"

"There you are!"

A woman entered the garage and made a beeline for baby Rune. Fiona's elderly lobby attendant, Teddy, hustled behind her, chugging like a locomotive.

Rune swore. "That's my mother," he muttered. He raised his arms. "Help me down?"

Fiona's lip curled. "What?"

He gritted his baby teeth. "Help me down and *listen*."

Fiona stepped forward to slide her arms under the boy's armpits, grimacing as if he were made of snot, yellow poo, and common cold viruses, which she assumed he *was*.

"I've regained my consciousness," he said as she pulled him from the hood of her car. "I'll be back the next chance I get, and we'll plot our path going forward."

She held him as he dangled in front of her. "Plot our path forward? What? You want me to help you fill out pre-school applications?"

Rune scowled, which would be an *adorable* expression on such a tiny face if Fiona didn't find children, in general, repulsive.

"For your information, I start first grade next week," he said.

He seemed genuinely proud. Fiona assumed his adult memories and child's mind remained jumbled.

"Congratulations," she said.

He glanced over his shoulder. His mother was closing in on them.

"Look, I'll be able to get away—"

Fiona laughed. "And then what? You're going to throw diapers at people until they make you king?"

"I am fully potty-trained!" Rune roared. He kicked at Fiona, and she dropped him. He landed on his feet, but his little legs collapsed like noodles, and he ended up on his butt, red-faced and furious. Fiona stepped back for fear he'd lunge forward to bite her ankles.

"Oliver!" yipped his mother as she swept in and scooped the boy up from the ground. She glared at Fiona. "Were you trying to kidnap him?"

Fiona barked a laugh. "*Kidnap* him? Lady, I don't want your stupid kid. The little ass was sitting on my car."

The woman held Rune to her chest, rocking him back and forth as he hung like a ragdoll. "Oliver, what were you thinking? Why would you run away from Mommy like that?"

"Yeah, *Oliver*, what were you thinking?" asked Fiona.

"My name is *Rune*," said the boy, glaring at his mother as he tried to push away from her.

A flash of embarrassment crossed the mother's face as she caught Fiona's eye. "His name's Oliver," she explained. "A few months ago, he told us he wanted to be called *Rune*. Refuses to respond to any other name." She chuckled and threw in an overly-dramatic eye roll. "*Kids.*"

Fiona nodded. "Hey, just spitballing here, but did you ever consider *Oliver* might be a time traveler reborn as your child, who recently remembered who he *really* is and wants to get back to his nefarious plan to take over the world?"

The woman's jaw dropped open, her gaze locked with Fiona's, her hand tight around Rune's wrist.

"What is wrong with you?" she asked.

Fiona shrugged. "Just a thought."

The woman glanced at the doorman and dragged Rune back the way they'd come.

Rune glanced over his shoulder at Fiona as he tried to keep up with his stupid little feet.

"I'll be back," he called.

"Don't hurry," Fiona returned.

She glanced at Teddy, who remained standing dumbly beside her.

"Sorry about that, Miss Fiona," he said, looking sheepish.

Fiona pointed in the direction mother and child had disappeared.

"You keep that kid away from me," she said. "You see him again, you call the police."

Teddy nodded. "Yes ma'am."

Fiona turned and continued to her car.

It was official.

Daddy's back.

She flopped into her seat and shut the door.

This is not good.

CHAPTER TWO

One day earlier...

After delivering an unconscious Rune to the holding cells at the newly reconstructed Angeli headquarters, Arch Angelus Michael stopped to peruse their ancient library, hoping to shed light on the curious case of the corrupted Kairos.

How many of them were spreading ill-will instead of hope and inspiration? Was Rune an anomaly, or were the time-traveling Kairos, who were *supposed* to inspire kindness in humans, breaking bad everywhere? In every time?

Surely, some Angelus scribe had recorded more information about these mysterious beings. He *hated* not knowing more about the Kairos—corrupted or not. Up until a few months ago, he'd been under the impression he and his fellow Angeli were the only entities driven by an unidentified but *undeniable* impulse to protect humans.

It was a point of pride, really...

Then, some of the Angeli scholars started noticing *time* anomalies. Angeli didn't jump through time.

What could these ripples in the Earth's aura mean?

After a little poking around, they discovered the existence of time travelers, which they christened *Kairos*—a Greek word loosely translating to *right time*. He'd picked the title himself—it seemed these Kairos inspired goodness in people. Wherever they landed, good things bloomed.

They decided there was no reason to mess with the Kairos—they'd let them grow like medicinal herbs but keep an eye on them. This plan worked fine until the scholars started noticing *bad things* happening around the Kairos. Some of them seemed to be afflicted with the same plague the Angeli had recently suffered. This 'virus' made the Kairos inspire *evil* in people instead of good.

Michael knew it was time to step in. He'd have to—

"Um, Michael?"

A lesser Angel, a guard Michael recognized from dropping off Rune, appeared at the doorway of the library.

"Hm?"

The guard crossed his hands in front of him. "Um, Michael, sir, that prisoner you brought in—"

Michael slid the book he'd been scanning back onto the shelf. "He's awake?"

Excellent.

He had many questions for Rune. The Kairos, even the *good* ones—like the Highlander and the Hollywood group—didn't know *how* they operated or where they'd come from. Not even Luther, the one who'd suddenly appeared on their radar as a freshly minted Angelus.

One of their own.

He hadn't let on, but Luther made Michael *livid.*

He'd known the balance was off—that they needed to replenish their numbers—but to have an Angelus spontaneously *appear*—

Scandalous.

Who approved that?

With the other Angeli, he'd pretended Luther's transformation was all part of a master plan only he was privy to, but...

He'd lied.

Then he imprisoned Rune to observe and interrogate him. Rune reminded him of Seth—who'd been patient zero with their Angeli infections. He couldn't let what happened with Seth happen again.

He needed to know more.

He needed to be prepared.

Michael snapped from his thoughts to find the Angel still blinking at him from the doorway.

"He's awake?" he repeated, realizing he hadn't heard an answer. He walked forward to push past the man and head toward the holding cells.

As he strode the great hall with the Angel scurrying behind

him, he *still* didn't hear an answer.

He turned on the heel of his Italian leather loafers, and the guard trailing him stopped to avoid smacking into him.

"*He's awake?*" he repeated a third time.

The Angel looked terrified.

A bad feeling washed over Michael.

He hadn't noticed that expression on the Angel.

The guard swallowed. "Um, not exactly..."

"What does that mean? Is he *dead?*"

"Um—"

Michael's teeth gritted. "Say *um* again, and I will rip off your wings."

"Uh—"

Clenching a fist, Michael spun to continue his trek to the prison.

"Whatever it is, *show me*," he growled.

Michael phased through the prison's main door and stopped in front of Rune's cell.

Rune's *empty* cell.

He turned on the guard again.

"Where did you move him?" he asked.

The Angel shook his head.

"We *didn't...*"

Michael turned. "You're saying he's *gone?*"

"Um..."

Michael's attention shot down the hall to the prison's office. "*Video.*"

The Angel nodded and led the way to the office, where another Angel sat up at the sight of Michael.

"Show me the feed," said Michael.

The Angel tapped a few keystrokes.

The video of Rune in his cell started with the image of Michael and a guard dragging him inside to lay his unconscious body on the hard bed folded down from the wall.

He and the guard left.

Rune remained there.

"*Fast forward*," said Michael.

The guard complied.

Rune's hand moved to his head, and the guard resumed playing the feed.

Rune sat up. He scanned his cell, walked to the door, and peered into the hall. He returned to the bed to sit, his legs dangling over the side.

Feeling the stump where his metal arm had been, he sighed.

Michael noticed Rune's metal arm still sitting on a table in the corner of the guardhouse.

They hadn't even had time to catalog the man's *arm* before he escaped.

Mortifying.

He returned his attention to the video. Rune raised his working arm and pinched his nose between his thumb and index finger.

Michael squinted at the screen.

Is he...?

Rune's body jerked.

It jerked again.

He slumped back against the wall, and a moment later, he was gasping for air and coughing.

He sat up, shook his head, and pinched his nose again.

Three more times, he passed out only to awake gasping.

Michael glared at the guards. "You didn't hear any of this?"

They shook their heads.

"We might have heard him cough, but we didn't think..." The sitting guard motioned to the screen and trailed off.

On his fourth attempt, Rune passed out and then disappeared with a flash of light.

Michael gaped at the screen.

He killed himself by refusing to breathe.

He didn't think that was *possible.*

Speechless, Michael stormed from the prison.

Anne had questioned the wisdom of taking Rune prisoner. He couldn't let his girlfriend know her concerns had been justified.

She'd be *insufferable.*

CHAPTER THREE

Broch slid the last forkful of blueberry cobbler into his mouth as Anne Bonny finished sharing the story of her life as a pirate and then as a Sentinel, in the employ of the immortal Angeli.

She shared the abbreviated version, of course. She'd been alive for three hundred years, battling the sorts of monsters he and Catriona were only beginning to fight.

It had taken Anne three hundred years to win her fight against the corrupted Angeli, which didn't bode well for their new war with Rune and his ilk, but Broch wasn't one to dwell on the negative.

After all, maybe everything Anne had gone through would make it that much easier for them. Catriona and Anne had already discovered they had to combine their powers to essentially *reboot* Rune's corrupted lackey, Joseph. They had to work together.

Score one for the good Kairos.

"I don't know what to say," said Catriona as Anne finished her story. "That's *insane*."

Anne nodded. "I know. It's a lot."

Broch agreed and noticed how tired Catriona looked. It had been a long day. They'd rebooted Joseph—restarted him by draining away his energy so he could be reincarnated fresh—and captured Rune for Michael.

Broch hadn't *loved* the idea of handing Rune over to Michael—he'd have preferred the bastard stay far away from Catriona—but who was he to argue with an angel?

Michael knew what he was doing.

Anyway, Catriona was probably feeling the weight of her new responsibilities. She usually spent her day getting actors out of trouble. Now, she was saving the world from evil.

He had it easy, as all he had to do was protect Catriona. There wasn't anything he'd rather do.

Catriona caught him looking at her and smiled. "I'll have to tell all of Parasol Pictures' assets that I need them to stop getting in trouble so I can concentrate on saving the world."

He nodded. "Ah'm sure that willnae be a problem."

Catriona chuckled. "Yeah. Who's more reasonable than actors?"

Jeffrey, Anne's assistant, entered the room with Broch's father, Sean, in his wake. Broch straightened. It still made him happy seeing Sean. Growing up as an orphan in eighteenth-century Scotland, he'd thought his father was dead. How could he have known the old man was alive and well in twenty-first-century Los Angeles, acting as father to his future love?

"I think this one's yours," drawled Jeffrey before disappearing again.

Sean looked flustered. As head of security at Parasol Pictures, he'd been the one to report Rune's trespassing to Catriona.

He hadn't known the disturbance was *Rune.*

"What are you doing here?" asked Catriona. "I thought you were having dinner with Luther?"

Sean released a breath as if he'd been holding it for the last hour. "I saw you and Broch on the security cameras chasing Rune. I came as fast as I could. When I couldn't find you, and you didn't answer your phone, I called Anne, and Jeffery let me know you were here."

Catriona frowned. "Shoot. Sorry. I should have called." She motioned to the robe she'd borrowed from Anne while her clothes dried. "I don't know if you saw, but I fell down the waterfall of the jungle set and into the pool there."

Sean's eyes widened. "*No*, I didn't see that. Are you okay?"

"I'm fine, but my phone didn't live through it."

Sean ran a palm over his hair. "So, it's done? You rebooted Rune?"

Catriona shook her head. "Not exactly. Michael took him."

"Took him where? Don't they need you and Anne to fix him?" Sean looked to Anne for answers.

"Michael wanted to question him first," said Anne.

Broch could tell by her tone she didn't love the angel's

decision, either.

Sean grunted, and Broch crossed his arms against his chest.

So, it's unanimous.

"Well, at least you two are okay," said Sean.

Catriona yawned.

Broch squeezed her hand beneath the table.

"It's late. Ah ken we should gae home," he suggested in a whisper. "Yer clothes are probably dry."

She nodded, and the two of them pushed back their chairs.

"We're going to head home," she announced. "I'm going to grab my clothes."

She left the room.

Sean sighed. "Me, too. I'm going to stay at Luther's." He perked as if he'd remembered something and motioned to Broch. "Hey, could I talk to you for a second?"

Broch nodded and said his goodbyes to Anne before following Sean out front.

"You two are okay?" asked Sean, heading toward where his truck sat in Anne's large driveway. "She's okay? She doesn't always tell me the truth."

Broch nodded. "Aye. We had a few dicey moments, but it all turned oot in the end."

"Good, good." Sean opened his car door and reached inside to pull out a small box.

"This is for you," he said, handing it to Broch.

Broch opened the lid.

Inside, nestled in tufted silk, sat a gold ring.

He looked at Sean. "Whit's this?"

"It's your mother's wedding ring," said Sean. "I thought maybe you'd like to give it to Catriona when you're ready."

Broch gaped at the golden band. "Ah dinnae ken whit tae say..."

Sean dismissed his concerns with a wave. "It sits in a drawer at my house. You should have it. There's an inscription on the inside..."

Broch plucked the ring from the box and peered at the inner band.

Mo Ghràdh, Mo Cuishle.

"My love, the pulse of my heart," he translated aloud.

Sean nodded, his lips pressed into a hard line. His eyes looked shiny.

Broch slipped the ring back into its box and clapped his

arms around his father.

"Ta, da."

"You're welcome." Sean squeezed him back, and they rocked like wrestling bears.

"What are you two up to?" asked a redressed Catriona as she headed down the driveway towards them.

The men separated, and Broch slipped the ring box behind his back.

"Just glad you're both okay," said Sean, wiping his eye.

Catriona squinted at them. "What a couple of softies."

They shrugged.

"I'll see you," said Sean, getting into his vehicle.

Catriona and Broch watched him go and then headed to her Jeep to make the short ride back to the studio lot.

"I'm tired," she said, yawning again.

He nodded.

"Me, tae."

They parked at Parasol Pictures and headed to their apartments above the payroll office. As they approached Catriona's apartment, she turned and slipped her arms around his neck.

"Stay with me tonight," she whispered.

He swallowed, the weight of the ring heavy in his pocket. His hands slipped around her waist as she slid against him like they were matching puzzle pieces.

Ah could give the ring tae her tonight...

But they were tired. And he'd sworn he wouldn't be with her until they were married—he'd already slipped once—but, *still*, it would be better if he got some sleep—

She stood on her toes and nibbled his neck below his ear.

"Aye," he said.

She's a siren. Ah cannae resist. It isnae my fault.

She opened the door to her apartment, and he kissed her before slipping from her grasp.

"Ah'm goin' tae get a shower," he said.

"I'll join you," she replied.

He spun on his heel. "*Na*—Ah mean, ah need a moment alone."

He winced.

Please don't ask why.

She shrugged, though she seemed a bit confused. "Okay."

He nodded, relieved.

Entering Catriona's bedroom, he shut the door behind him.

Whew.

He *did* want to get a shower, but he also wanted a moment to figure out the best way to ask for her hand. *Officially.* Once and for all and with an actual ring.

He hid the ring box behind the towels in the closet and hopped into the shower. By the time he'd finished, he thought he had the right words in his head. He put on the spare kilt Catriona had bought him in an attempt to keep him from wearing his good, *worn-in,* original kilt and fixed his hair *just sae.*

He shook a finger at himself in the mirror.

Dinnae cry.

He reached into the closet to find the ring box. Taking a deep breath, ring box in his hand, he opened the door and stepped into the living room.

"Cat—"

He stopped and scanned the room.

Catriona was gone.

Where...?

The room wasn't big enough for someone to hide in.

A strange snuffling noise reached his ears, and he cocked his head.

Snoring?

He took a few steps forward to find Catriona lying on the sofa, dead asleep, jaw open, a little spit on the corner of her mouth.

He smiled.

Ah well.

He lay a blanket over her and returned to the bedroom. He hid the ring deep behind the sweaters he'd never seen her wear and stripped down for bed.

Marital bliss had waited this long.

It could wait another day.

CHAPTER FOUR

Catriona snorted herself awake and scanned the room through half-staff eyelids.

My living room.

Why am I in the living room?

She sat up, and a blanket slid to the floor. She remembered now. She'd been on the sofa waiting for Broch to shower and must have fallen asleep. No doubt, he'd covered her with the blanket.

She stood and padded into the bedroom to find Broch asleep in the bed. She wiggled his exposed big toe.

"Hey, Kilty, wake up. We have to get to Anne's to start our training."

His eyes fluttered open, and he grinned.

"Guid mornin' bonny girl."

"I fell asleep on the sofa," she said.

He nodded. "Ye did."

"My turn to get a shower."

"Aye," he said, rolling over. "Ah'll sleep a wee mair."

Catriona took a shower and found the bulk of the bruises she'd gathered during the previous night's Rune hunt had healed. She always knew she was a fast healer, but now that she knew she was a Kairos, *everything* made more sense. It wasn't her imagination—she actually had some mild rapid-healing superpowers.

Pretty cool.

She wasn't sore or tired. She felt *fantastic*. They'd caught Rune. That was *huge*. Today, Anne would teach her all her fighting tricks in case they ran into more bad guys like Rune.

Things felt right between her and Broch, now that she'd stopped resisting his charms and given into the idea they were fated to be together.

Yep, things were looking pretty darn good.

She got dressed and found Broch fiddling around the kitchen sink. He was acting weird, but she didn't have time to figure out what he was up to. Sometimes, he fixated on modern conveniences. Maybe he'd discovered dish soap.

"I'm going to run my loop. You be ready by the time I come back, Kilty," she warned him.

He nodded. "Aye."

She kissed him and left to hop into a studio golf cart to make her official morning security rounds around Parasol Pictures.

Saving the world was still her side hustle. Protecting Parasol paid the bills.

For the next hour, she was going to be *normal Catriona.* Sean and Luther continued as the heads of security at Parasol, so she had to get back to work, too. She looked forward to running into a drug-addled actor or an actress with a gambling addiction...

She was going to play *normie* for an hour and then scoop up Broch and go to Anne's for Kairos reboot training.

She chuckled to herself.

Ridiculous.

Her life was ridiculous.

But it *was* exhilarating.

She slowed when a young woman raised her hand as if to hide her face as she walked past her golf cart.

"Whitney?"

The girl glanced at her and lowered her hand. Catriona could see she'd been crying.

"What's wrong?" she asked.

The girl sighed. "Nothing. I'm being too sensitive."

"No, seriously, what is it?"

Whitney sighed. "Huck Carter. He's got some skinhead biker gang group going on tonight, and they were giving me shit."

"Huck—?" Catriona knew the name. The man was a scourge. He and his show *The Other Side* gave fringe groups a voice on national television—groups who didn't *deserve* a voice in any civilized society.

Interviewing horrible people was always good for ratings.

But, Parasol didn't own *The Other Side*. The show belonged to another network.

"Wait, I have questions," said Catriona. "Why is Huck filming *here?*"

Whitney's eyes widened. "You didn't hear? We have his show now."

"*What?*" Catriona couldn't wrap her head around the news. Parasol's president was Aaron *Rothstein,* and Huck practically specialized in Nazis.

She looked at Whitney, hoping to find answers there. "Why would Aaron want that vermin on his lot?"

The girl shrugged. "We're all horrified, but everything comes down to money, as usual."

Catriona slumped back in her seat. She'd gone away for *one day* to deal with Kairos issues, and the studio hired a hate-monger.

Not that they ever check in with me before making decisions, but still...

She returned her attention to Whitney. "Are *you* okay? What did these creeps do?"

Whitney hugged her clipboard to her chest and rolled her eyes. "They didn't *do* anything. It's what they *said.*" She pursed her lips. "I'd rather not repeat it."

"No. That's fine. I'm sorry. If you'd like to file a complaint—"

Whitney shook her head. "I'll be fine. I'll see you, Cat."

She walked on, and Catriona watched her go.

This isn't right.

No matter how many advertising dollars they attracted, she couldn't have her employees hassled by neo-Nazis.

She hit the gas and headed to Aaron's office. Kiki, Aaron's receptionist and Sean's occasional girlfriend, looked up from her desk as she entered.

"What brings you here?" asked Kiki.

Catriona motioned to Aaron's inner office. "Is he in?"

"Yep. Just a sec."

Kiki hit the intercom and let Aaron know he had a visitor.

"Let her in," he responded.

With a nod from Kiki, Catriona entered Aaron's inner sanctum.

"Why is Huck Carter here?" she asked. No reason to beat around the bush.

"Whoa, slow down," said Aaron. He frowned. "*Hello* to you, too."

"Hello. Why the hell would you buy *The Other Side?*"

He frowned. "I'm not sure who the hell you think you are questioning my decisions, but if you must know, the man prints money."

"The man is a menace at best and *dangerous* at worst."

Aaron leaned back in his chair. "Again. I'm sorry. I missed the meeting where we decided *you* have input on our shows."

Catriona grimaced. Anger wasn't working. Maybe she'd try to appeal to his emotions.

"Aaron, this doesn't feel like *you.*"

Aaron's expression pinched as if he were growing angrier, so she rushed to her next point before he could stop her.

"I'm trying to understand. You're *Jewish.* As we speak, he's got a bunch of neo-Nazi skinheads on the lot harassing the employees."

Aaron appeared surprised—almost confused—but the fury she'd sensed building seemed to swallow any potential regret.

"Deal with it. That's why I have you—to fix problems on the lot. I'm at the end of my patience with this." He motioned to the exit. "Close the door on your way out."

"This isn't right." Catriona grimaced. "For the record, *I* think this is a mistake."

"Noted."

She turned to leave.

"Hey, Cat," he called as she reached for the doorknob.

She pivoted, hopeful he'd reconsidered.

"Yes?"

"Um, Fiona Duffy. She's your sister? Am I right?"

"Yes, as it turns out. Why?"

"I was wondering, have you heard anything from her lately? I can't seem to get hold of her."

Catriona stared at him.

That's it.

Aaron and Fiona had had a fling while her conniving sister was finagling her way onto Parasol's roster of stars.

Fiona had *inspired* Aaron to buy *The Other Side* with her reverse Kairos powers. What show was better for sowing hate and chaos?

She *is* infected.

She'd sworn she wasn't, and Team Highlander had given her the benefit of the doubt. Plus, she seemed to have some powers useful for finding *other* infected Kairos.

But maybe keeping her around was causing more harm than good. Nothing explained Aaron's out-of-character decision—except his time with Fiona.

"Did Fiona tell you to bring Huck onboard?" she asked.

He scowled. "*No.* What are you talking about? She doesn't make decisions any more than you do."

She nodded and assumed people didn't *know* when they were being manipulated by Kairos for good or evil. Maybe her sister didn't even know what she was doing—after all, *she'd* never realized she was inspiring *good* things in people. She thought she was just good at calming sticky situations.

"If I see her, I'll let her know you're looking for her," she lied.

He grunted. "Thank you."

Catriona exited and offered a quick goodbye to Kiki before hopping back on her golf cart and wheeling to where she'd seen Whitney. Retracing the direction the girl had come from, she found the set for *The Other Side* already set up on Soundstage Four.

Outside the building, three men in cliché biker clothing sat around a picnic bench, laughing with each other.

They watched as she approached.

"Ooh, boy, I think my ride's here," said one.

The other two laughed.

"Hey, dirtballs," said Catriona. "I'm going to need you to leave my people alone, do your interview, and get the hell off my lot."

"*Oooh,*" catcalled the group.

"She's *feisty,*" said one from his spot on the far side of the bench.

"I'd knock that right out of her," muttered another before spitting on the ground.

The man who'd first commented stood and walked toward her.

"I think *you* need a lesson in manners," he said, stopping inches from her.

Catriona stood her ground and poked a finger at the man.

"I hear another complaint, and you're *gone*."

He leaned forward. "Who's going to do that? *You?*"

The door on the soundstage opened, and Huck Carter stuck his head through the door.

"Oh, hey, guys, we're ready for you." He stepped into the sun and eyed Catriona. "You with them?"

Catriona snorted a laugh. "*Please.* I'm security. They were harassing the staff."

"Were they?" asked Huck, winking at the men. "Do you have a formal complaint to that effect?"

"Yeah, do you have a warrant?" said the man in the back, setting off a chain of guffaws from the others.

"Yeah, sweet thing," said the one closest to her. He raised his hand as if he were about to stroke her cheek. "Why don't you—"

Catriona chopped upward, shoving the man's hand into his nose. He yelped and stumbled back.

"You f—"

He bounced off the man behind him and raised his hand as if to strike Catriona.

Huck stepped in, doing his best to get between them without putting himself in actual danger.

"Whoa, whoa, *whoa*, guys. Everyone calm down."

Catriona kept her fists balled and ready. They were a distraction. She was better with her feet. She'd been about to make sure the oaf never used his right knee again.

Huck motioned to the men. "Why don't you three head into the studio and let me talk to…Miss, uh…"

"Catriona," she said.

"Miss *Catriona*."

"I'm supposed to let that go?" asked the leader as blood seeped from his nose.

"Aren't you on parole?" asked Huck.

The man grunted and headed into the studio. The others followed.

Huck turned to bless Catriona with his oily grin. "Well, it was nice to meet you, Miss Catriona, but I'd watch yourself around these big boys. I might not be here next time to save that pretty face of yours."

As Catriona glared at the rat of a man before her, a strange feeling passed over her.

He's one of them.

She didn't know how she knew. Alarms didn't go off, she didn't tingle with Spidey-sense—but she felt it to the marrow of her bones. It was almost as if he had a bit of a shimmer around him.

Am I imagining that?

Her opportunity to respond to his demeaning comments had passed. He'd assumed he'd scored—left her speechless—and turned to enter the studio.

He couldn't read her mind.

He didn't know she was formulating a plan.

She couldn't trust her instinct. She couldn't *assume* Huck was a corrupted Kairos.

She needed a Kairos detector.

Hm.

Maybe it was time to check in on Sis.

CHAPTER FIVE

Fiona knocked on the door of Dr. Peter Roseum's office—Doctor "Noseeum," as he was known on the Parasol Pictures lot, thanks to his vault-like ability to keep the medical secrets of the rich and famous.

"Come in," called Pete.

Fiona entered, pleased to see the little man smile at the sight of her. *Poor thing.* She could fit three of him into one Broch. The doc had a crush on her sister, but he didn't stand a chance with Catriona as long as the Plaid-Skirted Beefcake was around.

"Hey, Fiona," he said, ducking and covering his head with his hands. "Should I be on the lookout for flying darts?"

"I think you're safe this time," she said, perching across from where he sat at his desk.

The last time they'd been together, her father's weirdo henchmen had shot Noseeum with a blow dart and kidnapped Fiona. Joseph, a.k.a. *weirdo henchman*, was dead. Or *gone*. She wasn't entirely sure how it worked when "corrupted" Kairos were "rebooted" by "good" Kairos, like her sister, and sent into the aether to "heal."

She needed to look into that.

The whole thing sounded sketchy at best. She wasn't sure the good guys even bought it.

But, on the upside, they hadn't rebooted *her*. She wasn't sure why not. She'd told them she wasn't infected, of course, but she didn't know if it was *true* or why they would believe her. She didn't *think* she was infected—she was just *her*. She *did* seem to be able to talk people into things sometimes. She wanted power and money and fame, but that only made her like every other actor in Hollywood.

Sure, she'd encouraged the previous owner of her apartment to blow up his life so she could get his place, but...

It was a *nice* place.

It didn't mean she had some evil superpower.

Necessarily.

She did *want* to know, though. That's why she'd come up with a little plan for Noseeum.

"So, what's up? How are you doing after your kidnapping?" asked Pete.

"I'm good, but I had a lot of time for thinking, and it occurred to me that you and I have a common goal."

He perked. "Oh yeah? What's that?"

"Breaking up Catriona and Broch."

The amused smile on Pete's lips died. "I don't want to break them up—"

"Yes, you do."

Fiona reached out to take Pete's hand in hers. She concentrated. *Really* concentrated. She'd never tried so hard to sway someone before.

Pete swallowed. His gaze seemed trapped by hers.

"Um... Out of curiosity, what did you have in mind?"

She stroked the back of his hand.

"I'm not sure. Why don't you keep the thought in the front of your mind and let me know what hits you? In the meantime, I'll be thinking on it, too."

"Why, uh, why do you want to break them up?"

She shrugged. "It's complicated."

She didn't need to tell Pete she wanted them distracted by heartache so they'd forget about her. If their minds were on other things, she wouldn't have to worry about them lurking around trying to reboot her.

Plus, while Pete was moving in on Catriona, *she* wouldn't mind a run at the Highlander. The man was ridiculously gorgeous.

She wasn't sure how helpful Pete would be, but the doctor was one of the few people Catriona might confide in.

Pete slid his other hand on top of hers. "Are you after Broch? Because you and I were on our way to dinner when we were so rudely interrupted by your kidnapping—"

She frowned. "I don't want to be your substitute for Catriona. You know she's the one you want."

"Do I?"

Fiona squeezed his hand and tried harder. Seems she wasn't so much mesmerizing him as she was *turning him on.*

He huffed. "You're right. I'm sorry. I'm tired of being in the *friend zone.* She needs to recognize who I am."

"*Exactly,*" said Fiona.

Pete continued, a fire igniting in his eyes. "I've always been there for her. All those *dates* of hers I've listened to her talk about—"

Fiona sniffed. "How *dare* she."

"*Exactly.* How *dare* she use me like that?"

Fiona felt anger radiating off of him in waves.

He certainly seems inspired.

Maybe she *was* influencing him, but she wasn't ready to call herself *infected.* Mostly, she wanted to know how Rune had drained energy from people to heal himself—

She straightened.

Ooh. If I can figure out that trick and make myself look younger, I can start a beauty line and sell the shit out of it to idiots hoping to look as good as me...

She felt giddy thinking about it.

The *real* money was in lifestyle brands.

She'd figure it out. After all, *Rune* figured it out, and he was damn near insane—had been for as long as she could remember.

She closed her eyes and tried to pull Pete's life force from his hand.

"Are you okay?" asked Pete.

She opened her eyes. He was peering at her, clearly unaffected.

Ah well. It was worth a shot.

She patted his hand again before standing.

"Hey, Pete, have you ever considered being an expert spokesperson for a line of beauty products?"

His brow knit. "Huh?"

She sniffed. "Never mind. I'll catch you later."

Fiona strode out of the office feeling reenergized.

Maybe it would be worth the risk to ask baby Rune if he could train me how to—

She stopped dead. A familiar man leaned against the building across from Noseeum's, his hands in his pockets.

His gaze was locked on *her.*

What was his name again?

Con.

He was one of those Sentinels who worked for the Angeli—like the redhead who had combined powers with Catriona to send Joseph away. *Anne what's-her-face.*

Fiona's heart quickened into another gear. A hunger came over her. Con didn't have the *money* feel of Michael the Angel, but he *did* have an undeniable animal magnetism—

"Hello, you..." she said, strolling toward him.

He grinned. "Hullo."

He liked what he saw. She could tell.

"To what do I owe this pleasure?" she asked.

"I've been tasked to keep an eye on ye." He smirked. "I've had worse jobs."

She looked him up and down as if he were a side of beef and she hadn't eaten in weeks.

"How *close* of an eye do you need to keep on me?" she purred.

He didn't flinch.

"*Close*," he said. "I need to stay on top of ye."

She motioned behind her. "My apartment's down the street. Care to follow me there?"

He licked his lips and smiled.

"Don't mind if I do."

CHAPTER SIX

Broch opened his eyes to find Catriona wiggling his toe.

"Guid mornin', bonny girl."

"I fell asleep on the sofa," she said.

He nodded, remembering. "Ye did."

"I'm going to get a shower."

She headed in the direction of the bathroom, and Broch heard the door shut.

A bolt of panic ran through him.

The ring.

He scanned the room around him.

Where did I put it?

Jogging to the closet, he felt behind Catriona's sweaters until his fingers touched the box.

Whew.

He opened the lid to find the ring nestled in its place. He squinted at it.

It looked cloudy.

Fingerprints.

Scowling, he tucked the box back under the sweaters and took the ring into the kitchen to rinse it off. He wasn't sure how to clean gold, but he figured soap would work. The bottle of blue dish-cleaning liquid Catriona had was like *magic.*

The modern world was full of wonders.

On a top-ten list of his favorite things in the twenty-first century, *soap* accounted for four of them. Soap that removed grease. Soap that smelled amazing. Soap that made his hair fluffy. There was soap in the seventeenth and eighteenth centuries, of course, but nothing like this stuff.

Twenty-first-century soap was the *best*.

Catriona was still number one on his favorites list, but shampoo was a close second.

Finding a dishcloth, he turned on the water and let it run across the gold ring.

"What are you doing?"

Broch jumped. The ring squirted from his wet fingers and flew into the air before dropping directly down the sink drain with a muffled *clink*. He gasped.

"What's wrong?" Catriona moved towards him, dressed in jeans and that confounded *bra*, brushing her teeth.

He turned his back to the sink to block her view. "Nothing."

She scowled, and he knew he'd have to be more proactive if he was going to keep her from investigating.

"Whit are *ye* doan?" he asked.

"I'm going to spit," she mumbled through foaming lips as she moved toward him.

"Na."

Her frown deepened. "What?"

"The sink in the bathroom is fer spit." He pointed towards the bedroom. "Gae."

She rolled her eyes and headed that way. "Weirdo."

The moment she disappeared around the corner, Broch thrust his hand down the wide opening of the sink. After a few moments of fumbling around the slimy bottom, he felt something move.

Please be it.

He pinched the object and pulled it out.

The ring.

Thank God.

Catriona returned a moment later, eyes locked on her phone. He tucked the ring behind his back.

"I got a text from Anne. She said to come around eleven, so we have some time." She eyeballed him. "Better be ready by the time I come back, Kilty."

He nodded. "Aye."

She kissed him on the cheek, glanced side-eyed at the sink, and left.

Broch let out a sigh of relief.

Ah cannae get nothin' by her.

Luckily, she had things to do, or she would've delved into

why he was hovering around the sink. He was sure of that.

Broch found a dishtowel and shined the ring—away from the sink—before putting it back in its box and heading back to the bedroom to get dressed.

He'd barely slipped into his kilt before he heard a knock on the door.

Whit noo?

He opened it to find Catriona's friend, Dr. Pete, standing there.

"Oh," he said as Broch opened the door.

He seemed disappointed. Broch wasn't thrilled either. The two of them had been butting heads one way or the other since he showed up.

"Hullo, Pete."

The doctor eyed his kilt. "Why are you in your skirt?"

"T'is nae a skirt. T'is a *kilt*." Broch set the ring box on the kitchen island and began tucking in his shirt. He didn't have time to blether with the wee doctor.

"Whit dae ye need?" he asked.

"Nothing. I was looking for Cat—what's that?" He pointed at the box.

Broch paused. He couldn't help but smile. "It's a ring."

Pete swallowed. "What kind of ring?"

"A betrothment ring."

"For Catriona?"

Broch nodded. Realizing he'd forgotten his sporran, he held up a finger and jogged into the bedroom.

"Ah'm goan tae ask her tae marry me when she gets back," he said over his shoulder as he left.

He and Catriona were *technically* already husband and wife. They'd stopped in Las Vegas after a job as a joke and accidentally ended up *actually* married—but he'd never given her a ring, and he wanted to start over and do things *right*.

He located his pouch and headed back to the living room.

Maybe Pete would have some idea about the best way to ask for Catriona's hand. Folk probably did things differently now than they had in his day.

"Pete, dae ye have any ideas—?"

Re-entering the living room, Broch stopped.

The front door was open.

Pete was gone.

He looked at the counter.

The ring box was gone, too.

Broch heard the ding of the elevator and roared.

"Pete!"

Running into the hallway, he dashed to the elevator as the doors closed, too late for him to stop them.

Ah'm goan tae break his wee neck...

Bolting to the stairs, he pounded his way down, but by the time he'd burst into the lower office, Pete was already pushing through the front door to the world outside.

Jeanie, the woman who ran the payroll office, looked up from her desk, her hand planted on her chest.

"You two are going to scare me to death. Are you playing tag? You're in your kilt. Don't you look—"

Broch ran past her and outside. He spotted Pete heading into the bowels of the studio, where there were a million places to hide.

"Git back here, ye wee bastard!"

Broch sprinted after the doctor with a speed he didn't know he possessed. He found Pete, closed in, and snatched the thief by the back of his shirt collar, jerking the wee man to a stop that flipped him off his feet.

"Ack!" coughed Pete.

Worried he'd broken the man's trachea, Broch released him, and the doctor collapsed to his knees.

"You could have *killed* me," Pete wheezed.

"Sorry. Gimme the *ring.*"

Pete handed Broch the box and tried to crawl away on his hands and knees.

The highlander opened the box.

Empty.

Ye wee shite—

Broch grabbed Pete's retreating ankle and dragged him back.

Pete slapped his hand to his mouth as Broch flipped him over.

He swallowed.

Hard.

Broch gaped.

"Did ye just swallow mah ring?"

Pete nodded, looking half-defiant and half as if he was about to throw up.

Broch sneered.

He grabbed Pete's collar and pulled him to his feet. Placing a paw on the doctor's neck, he folded his flailing body in half, forcing his face to point at his knees.

"Get off me, you gigantic slab of *moron*," croaked Pete.

"Yer gonna spit it oot."

"No. *Never*."

Securing Pete in a headlock, Broch opened the man's jaw with one hand and pushed a finger down his throat with the other.

Pete tried to bite. Broch held his jaw.

"Ye bite me, ye wee terrier, ah'll pull yer insides oot!"

Pete gagged. Once. Twice.

He heaved.

Coffee-tinged water splashed to the ground.

Water, and one shiny gold ring.

Grimacing, Broch snatched the ring from the slop as Pete collapsed and rolled away, sputtering and wiping drool from his lips.

Broch studied the ring to be sure the wily imp hadn't pulled another switch on him. It had the inscription it should.

He glared at the doctor.

"Whit is *wrong* with ye?"

Pete's shoulders slumped as he tried to catch his breath. "I don't know."

"Ye just *ate* mah *ring*."

Pete shook his head. "I know, I *know*. I don't know what came over me. I couldn't bear the thought of you and Cat getting married, and I saw the box sitting there, and I—"

Broch clucked his tongue.

"We're already merrit."

Pete looked up. *"What?"*

"We're already *merrit*. In Las Vegas." He decided against admitting it was a joke wedding turned real. Soon, that wee detail wouldn't matter.

"But, you're giving her a ring *now*?"

"Ah didnae hae it then."

Pete rubbed his throat, pouting.

"Are ye okay?" asked Broch, suffering a twinge of regret at how he'd manhandled the wee doctor.

"Yeah. I guess." Pete sniffed. "I guess I'm going to have to kill you now."

Broch laughed.

"Ah dinnae think sae."

Pete sighed. "I'm kidding. I think. Help me up."

Ring safely tucked in one palm, Broch helped him to his feet.

"I'm going to go now. I might need a nap or something. I don't know what's wrong with me." He slapped Broch's arm. "I'm sorry."

Broch nodded.

Pete wandered off, his hands in his pockets, shoulders hunched.

Whit has gotten into that laddie?

He knew Pete was sweet on Catriona, but he'd never imagined the doctor could act so out of character. It wasn't that long ago he was on his way to a date with—

He gasped.

"*Pete!*" he called.

Pete turned, looking as if his best friend had just run away with his wife and his dog.

"Huh?"

"Hae ye been hanging out with Fiona? Catriona's sister?"

Pete scowled. "I saw her this morning. Why?"

Broch frowned.

"Nothin'. Gae on yer way."

Pete held his gaze a moment longer and then continued on his path.

Fiona.

She is evil.

He'd have to tell Catriona what happened but find some way to leave out the part about the ring.

He looked at the ring. The gold was cloudy again, this time with the contents of Pete's tummy.

Ah need mair soap.

CHAPTER SEVEN

"This is the best job I've ever had," said Con, rolling onto his back. Beside him, Fiona lay spent.

"What was *that*?" she asked, breathless.

"Hm?"

"That thing... at the end... It felt *amazing*."

Con leaned up on one elbow and cocked an eyebrow at her. "Ye never had a—"

"Not *that*," she said, laughing. "But *yes* that. It was *different*. More intense. Longer..."

"That's what she said," said Con. He never tired of that joke. Catriona did. She used to roll her eyes like craps dice every time he said it.

He paused as a flash of something ugly passed through him. He wanted to lash out—hit something, scream, *hurt someone*. He pressed his arms tight against his sides to keep from acting on the impulse.

Why?

He closed his eyes and braced against his violent urges.

"Con?" prompted Fiona.

"Just a second," he said through clenched teeth.

He tried to think happy thoughts and take deep breaths through his nose. After a few minutes, the sensation left him.

He relaxed.

Fiona put a hand on his shoulder. "Are you okay? You looked like you were in pain."

"No. I—" He didn't know how to explain the sensation to her and didn't feel like discussing it. He opted to change the subject.

"Um, what were we talking about?"

"You were going to explain to me what you did to me there at the end—"

"Oh. Right. Well, I'd like to take credit as the world's greatest lover. As it happens, when I gained my powers, it's something I inherited. Something the Angeli can do. They drain a little life out of you—it feeds them and, for you, feels good."

"*Good*?" scoffed Fiona. "That's an understatement."

He snorted a bitter laugh and put his hands behind his head. "Yeah, me and Michael used to fight for Anne's affections—back before I got me Angeli powers. Not exactly a fair fight when he could do *that*, eh? I had no idea."

"She's dated you *both*?"

He nodded.

"Lucky girl," she mumbled.

He turned to eye her. "I'm assuming you mean because of the *me* half of that equation."

"Oh, *absolutely*," she said, tickling him on his chest.

He blocked her as a strange thought passed through his mind.

I should wait until she falls asleep and then cut all her hair off.

He looked away, afraid she could read his mind.

Cor, where did that come from?

While he wasn't *straining* to prevent himself from exploding with anger anymore, whatever fit had overtaken him wasn't entirely expelled from his system.

Fiona continued, oblivious. "Explain your situation to me again? Are you an Angeli or a Sentinel like Anne?"

Con sniffed. "Long story, but I'm a little of both now. *Power*-wise. I'm not a dirty Angel, though. I'm still me, my own self." He looked at her. "Kind of like you, eh? Yer a mix-up. Not like the others—not like yer sister."

She closed her eyes and nodded. "Mm-hm. And not whatever my father is."

"Do you think it's a coincidence your family ended up together again? You, your sister, and your father?"

She shrugged. "I sensed Catriona."

"Hm?"

She sighed. "I can tell if other people are like me."

"You can track other Kairos?"

She shrugged. "I guess. Rune does it too. He found me. I

found Catriona. I guess it's hereditary."

Con sensed she was uncomfortable and let the conversation drop. She did as well. She closed her eyes, and he stared at the ceiling listening to her breathing slow until she fell asleep.

Stealing a little of her life force to give her a thrill had tuckered her out.

He'd seen it before.

Staring at her helpless form, strange new thoughts flooded his mind.

Superglue her skin.

Magic-Marker her face.

Trash her apartment.

Drain her into a coma.

Con scrambled out of bed and put his hands on his head.

Stop!

He found his clothes and left the room.

What is wrong with me?

Was she influencing him to be evil?

If she was, it didn't make sense. He'd been around her before. They all had, and no one had started breaking vases and kicking wheelchairs down staircases.

Was it the sex? Was her corruption some sort of sexually transmitted disease?

He pulled out his pants and peered inside.

Little Con appeared normal.

Whew.

He snapped his waistband closed. He'd figure it out later. For now, he needed to get away from Fiona and clear his mind before he did something *awful.*

Con sneaked out of her apartment and took the elevator downstairs. He rushed through the lobby, nearly knocking over a loitering boy as he fought to exit the building.

The boy spun and fell against a chair.

Con laughed and then slapped his hand over his mouth, horrified.

I'm the bloody devil.

He stepped outside and scooted around the corner, looked both ways to make sure no people or cameras were watching, and then shimmered into light to fly to Anne.

She'd know what to do.

Anne was sitting by the pool when Con materialized on the patio. She'd been reading an unputdownable thriller novel called *The Girl Who Wants* because what *she* wanted was *some quiet time.*

Naturally, Con showed up.

Having friends who appeared like magic without notice—and who didn't seem to consider it *rude*—was an ongoing problem in her life.

She scowled at him. "What are you doing here? You're supposed to be watching Fiona."

"She's asleep," he said, looking distracted.

"Are you sure?"

"I'm sure."

He pulled his shirt over his head and faced the pool as if preparing to dive in.

Scratches crisscrossed his back. It looked as if he'd been thrown into a pit of angry wolverines.

She put her Kindle aside and sat up.

"What happened to you? Did you lose a bet with a thrasher?"

He turned. "Hm?"

"You've got scratches all over your—" She gasped as the truth dawned on her. "*No.* You *didn't—*"

He touched his shoulder and then grinned.

"Oh, aye. I *did.*"

Anne dropped her head into an open palm. "Why? You don't find sex with your *target* a conflict of interest?"

"It was a conflict, all right," he said, chuckling. "The woman is *wild.*"

"*The woman* might be someone we have to *eradicate* later. Did you think of that? I don't need you hesitating at a crucial moment because you're picturing her naked."

He held up his palm as if asking her to wait. The muscles in his jaw flexed. His fingers curled into fists.

It looked as if he'd been struck by a wave of heartburn. Could it be *guilt*? *Shame*?

Ha. That'll be the day.

"What's wrong?" she asked.

He took a deep breath and seemed to *force* a smile on his face.

"Nothin'. No troubles. Me and Fiona are strictly business." He winked. "*Naughty* business."

Anne shook her head. "You're unbelievable," she muttered, but she kept an eye on him. His joke seemed strained. Usually, quips flowed from him like carbon dioxide.

"What's wrong with you? What was that look on your face? Are you sick?"

He frowned. "It's something I wanted to talk to you about—"

She waved him toward the pool. "First, heal those scratches. If Michael sees—"

"If Michael sees what?" said Michael, phasing through the slider to the patio.

Anne grimaced.

These people always popping in and out...

Con flashed, disappearing and then reappearing, his back now blemish free. He held out his hands as if he were trying to keep his balance aboard a ship tossed in a stormy sea. Anne scowled. That bobble was something new as well.

What's going on with him?

Michael cocked his head. "What are you two up to?"

"Just a swim." Con straightened his arms and fell back into the pool, hitting the water with a smack.

Anne winced at the sound. A moment later, the Irishman surfaced, sputtering.

"That hurt more than I expected," he said.

Michael sighed as he sat beside Anne.

"Are your students here?" he asked.

"Not yet. Eleven." She couldn't put her finger on it, but something about Michael felt *off* as well. She'd taken two minutes to enjoy a good book, and the world had tilted on its axis.

"What's going on with you?" she asked.

He shrugged. "Hm? Nothing."

"You seem *off*."

"Me? No..."

She took his hand in hers. "I'm your girlfriend. You know by law you have to tell me if something's up, right?"

His expression soured as if he'd caught a whiff of rotten

egg. "*Girlfriend*? Can't we find a better word? That sounds so *juvenile*. Lover?"

Anne barked a laugh. "*Lover?* Come on. No one says, Hey, I'd like you to meet my *lover*."

"Paramour?"

Anne pinched the bridge of her nose. There was something to be said for the uncomplicated romance she'd shared with Con—

"Check it out," called Con from the pool. He strained like a baby taking his first poopy, and bubbles popped to the surface around him.

He giggled. "Instant hot tub!"

Anne hung her head.

I really need to expand my dating pool...

"Hey, um, we agree that the Kairos time travel when they die, right?" asked Michael.

Anne focused on him. It was odd he hadn't bothered to insult Con for being infinitely less refined than himself.

Very odd.

Even his question was strange. Michael never admitted to not knowing *everything.*

"Yes, from what we've gathered." She paused to study Michael, but he kept his eyes averted, nodding his head slowly as if his thoughts were elsewhere.

Hm.

"Speaking of Rune, have you gotten anything out of him?" she asked.

Michael snapped from his trance. "Hm? No. Not yet. Um, with the time-traveling—wasn't there a difference if they're *dying* versus if they're *dead*?"

"If they're *dying*, they time-jump and continue as-is in a different time. Their wounds heal, though more slowly if they were inflicted by a fellow Kairos. If they *die*, they're reborn in another time as a baby and are forced to start over."

"That's what happened to Catriona?"

"Right. That's why she doesn't have much memory of her time *before* this time."

"But Brochan does?"

"Some. He says it comes back to him in dribs and drabs. Rune seems to remember everything, always, no matter how many times he comes back."

"And he can jump with *precision*?"

"Right. The others show up somewhere new with little to no control over where."

Michael tongued the inside of his cheek. "Luther says he has some control, but not like Rune."

"Maybe it has something to do with how old they are or how many times they've jumped." Anne shrugged. "Mind if I ask why we're going over what we *know* instead of getting *new* information out of Rune?"

"I, uh..." Michael looked away again as Con stepped out of the pool. "I don't know. Just taking a break."

"Uh-huh."

Anne didn't believe a word of it. In three hundred years, she could count the times she'd heard Michael say *I don't know* on one hand, and they were usually about whether or not they were officially dating.

"You know what we need?" said Michael. He pulled at his chin like a television detective deducing the solution to a murder.

Michael was a terrible actor.

Fine. I'll bite.

"What?" she asked as Con strolled toward them, drying his floppy locks with a towel.

"We need a way to hunt corrupted Kairos."

Con stopped drying.

"I got you, Champ," he said.

Michael scowled. "Do *not* call me *Champ*."

Con shook his head. "No, seriously. I can help, Sport."

Michael stood as if he were going to leave.

"No, wait, how can you help?" Anne asked Con. As usual, the men would rather measure...*wings*...than act like adults and help each other.

Con shrugged. "Easy. *Fiona.*"

"What about her?"

"She can sense other Kairos."

Anne shrugged. "We suspect that but—"

"No. *For certain.* She told me."

"Why would she tell *you*?" asked Michael.

Con smiled and glanced at Anne. She shook her head as subtly as possible.

"Accidentally," said Con. "She just screamed—I mean, *blurted* it out."

"I need to talk to her," said Michael, blessedly oblivious to Con's innuendo. The scowl he had permanently pointed in the Irishman's direction deepened. "Aren't you supposed to be watching her?"

"She's sleeping."

Michael looked at his watch. "At eleven?" He clucked his tongue with disapproval.

So easy for a man who never needed to sleep to consider people who did *lazy*.

"You should get back to Rune," Anne told Michael. She didn't imagine Con could keep himself from saying something stupid for much longer. He *loved* getting a rise out of Michael, and he was *stunningly* good at it. "I have to get ready for Catriona and Broch."

Michael nodded. "Yes. Keep me updated. I want to talk to Fiona *today*. Make it happen."

Con saluted. "Aye aye, Captain."

Michael's electric blue wings expanded, flashing a moment before he disappeared.

Not before he uttered a final word.

"*Idiot*."

When he was gone, Anne looked at Con. "She said that? She confirmed she can track them?"

"She did." His lips twisted into a knot. "But, there's another thing I wasn't ready to tell the Angel."

"What's that?"

"I think I might be able to draw the evil out of her."

Anne blinked at him. "Dare I ask what that means?"

"After we were, uh, you know—"

"Got it."

"She was suddenly, I don't know...*softer*. And I—" He shook his head. "Let's just say the stuff going through my head was *not* nice."

Anne's eyes widened. "Are you saying *you're* being infected?"

He shook his head. "No. It didn't last long. I had a few nasty thoughts about Michael after he showed up, but I always do. I think it's worn off. I feel normal. My healing probably helped."

Anne nodded. It made sense. Kind of. In her world.

"Does this *softening* make her more receptive to suggestions? Can you manipulate her, for lack of another word—"

He grinned. "Oh, I can manipulate her all right, and she's *definitely* recep—"

"*Stop.*" Anne put a hand over Con's mouth. She considered the possibilities while he submitted to her makeshift gag, his eyes dancing with amusement.

"Is it only temporary? Or do you think you could have a permanent positive effect on her?"

She lowered her hand to allow him to answer.

He shrugged. "I don't know. I can chart my progress, I guess."

Anne nodded. "Good. Do that. And get her to come to see me ASAP."

"Even if I have to—"

Anne sighed.

"Whatever it takes."

CHAPTER EIGHT

Rune sat on the sofa in front of his cartoons, but he wasn't watching the television. His little feet stuck out in front of him, barely reaching the edge of the cushion.

A useless body.

He glared at his mother, Ashley Carter. His memories had returned, and she'd outworn her usefulness. She'd birthed him, nursed him, kept him alive during his most vulnerable moments in the new timeline—but he didn't need her anymore.

He rubbed his finger in the gap where his front tooth used to be. He'd just lost it.

I wonder...

In addition to his memories, his previous skills had returned. He was whole again in every way except one.

This stupid body.

Ashley noticed him staring at her.

"What are you doing?" she asked.

"Thinking," he said.

She chuckled. "You are such a weird kid. You don't want to watch cartoons anymore?"

"I never did."

"Oh, stop. You love these. Do you want to go read in your room?"

Rune slid off the sofa and walked to her.

He lifted his arms.

"What are you doing?" she asked.

"I want to sit in your lap."

She smiled. "You do? Aww, sweet boy, you never want to snuggle."

She pulled him on her lap, and he wrapped his arms around her neck.

"Are you okay? Does your tummy hurt?" she asked.

He felt the smooth skin of her nape against his tiny palms.

Let's see.

Concentrating, he *pulled* from her.

She gasped.

"*Oliver—*"

As her life force flowed into him, she stood. He clung to her like a chubby-cheeked remora eel.

"Get off of me," she said as the panic rose in her voice. "You're hurting Mommy."

She swung, and his feet lifted into the air. As she stumbled, he locked his legs around her waist. He kept hold of her, hungry for the flesh-on-flesh contact he had to maintain to finish her.

Her panic grew. She beat on him, trying to wrench him away, but he grew stronger. He tightened his grip, pulling himself against her and pressing his cheek against her chest. She fell to her knees and collapsed forward, banging his spine against the coffee table. He cried out.

That hurt.

He held.

A moment later, she burst into dust.

He collapsed to the floor, a cloud of particles swirling above his head.

Coughing, he stood and brushed himself off. He felt *amazing,* like he always did after devouring human energy.

He felt different in another way, too.

Rune walked into the master bathroom and closed the door to peer into the mirror mounted to the back.

He was older. Maybe by three or four years. His clothes had ripped from his body and hung in tattered clumps.

It worked.

He'd concentrated on aging during the length of his feed. In the past, he only fed to heal an injury. After a while, he lost his taste for normal food and fed on human energy for nourishment. This time, he'd fed to speed the aging process.

He had to make up for his horrible miscalculation of time.

He was becoming a *god.*

Rune returned to the living room and found the remote control. Flipping through the channels, he spotted a clip from his father's program.

Huck Carter was doing good work. He'd made the transition from respected journalist to chaos-reaping sensationalist in three years.

He had access to Parasol Pictures, where the Highlander hid from Rune.

Huck was a valuable pawn.

CHAPTER NINE

Broch knew he'd have to tell Catriona what happened. Pete had acted completely out of character, and the only explanation was the time the wee man had spent with Fiona. They'd suspected Fiona was sick, and the doctor's actions seemed to confirm it.

But how could he tell Catriona without revealing the existence of the ring?

Broch headed in the direction of the apartments, his attention drifting to a soundstage production of what Catriona had called a 'Lord of the Rings Knockoff.' Whatever that meant. He'd seen a giant box of rings there during his security rounds a few days earlier, and the memory gave him an idea.

They ken how tae clean rings.

Broch shifted direction and wandered through the studio until he spotted a woman sitting next to the vat of golden rings, all of them similar to the one in his hand—simple gold bands. The woman was threading the bands onto some sort of clear string.

She glanced at him as he entered, and he held out his ring.

"Hullo. Ah wis wonderin' if ye could help me clean this—"

The woman snatched the ring from his hand and tossed it into the vat with the others before returning to her work.

Broch stood, stunned.

"Whit did ye *dae*?" he asked.

"Hm?"

Broch moved to the tub of rings and scanned the collection with a growing sense of dread.

"That wis *mah* ring."

The woman glanced up. "Huh?"

"*That wis mah ring.* Ah'm goan tae ask Catriona tae marry

me."

She gaped. "Wait. Are you saying I threw *your* engagement ring in there?"

"*Aye.*"

She gasped and covered her mouth. "Oh my God, I'm *so* sorry." She stood to peer into the vat. "I thought you *found* it. I thought one of these had gotten away from me."

Broch scowled. "*Na.*"

The woman dragged her hand across the pile of golden bands. "Okay. Okay. It couldn't have gone far. What did it look like?"

Broch lifted a random ring from the pile. "Like *this*."

"Is there any way we can tell which is yours?"

"It has an inscription inside."

She seemed relieved to hear. "Okay. Ours don't. That's something."

"And there's boak all over it."

Her features drew into a tight knot in the middle of her face. "It has *what* on it?"

"Boak. Er, vomit."

"Really?"

He nodded. "Long story."

She heaved a sigh and bellied up to the vat.

"I guess there's only one way to do this."

One by one, they picked through the rings. Whenever someone walked within earshot, the woman called them over and asked for help until they had half a dozen men and women picking through the pile.

Broch was starting to lose hope when a young blond woman yipped.

"I found it!"

She held it aloft like a trophy.

"Does it look like there's barf all over it?" asked the prop lady.

"What? *Ew.*" The blonde's lip curled as she dropped it back into the vat.

Broch saw it fall and snatched it up. He checked for the inscription.

It was there.

He released a great sigh and held it toward the prop lady, his grip on it *tight*.

"Kin ye clean it? That's whit ah came tae ask ye."

She held out her palm for him to drop the ring into it.

"That's not what I do," she said, grimacing, "but I guess I owe you that much."

Broch made his way back to Catriona's apartment with his freshly cleaned ring. Inside the apartment, he tested various poses, readying himself and running through his proposal.

Left leg forward.

Right leg forward?

One knee.

Both knees?

Fighting monsters like Rune was a walk down a country lane on a summer's day compared to asking Catriona to sign off on her love for him.

He wiped his forehead.

Howfur am ah sweating?

He didn't want any more confusion over the legitimacy of their wedding. This would be—

Catriona walked through her front door while he was in the middle of a deep knee bend. He straightened, and she stopped, staring at him.

"What are you doing?" she asked.

He hemmed. "Nothin'?"

"You're in your kilt."

"Aye."

There was a pause as they stared at each other. Broch fingered the box behind his back, nerves dancing.

"You remember we have to go to Anne's for training, right? Are you sure you want to wear that?"

He could tell by her tone that she wasn't thrilled at the idea.

Broch shrugged. "Na?"

"Okay. Change. We need to go." Catriona closed the door behind her and paused to cock her head at him. "Is there something wrong? You look...*weird*."

He swallowed.

'Tis because ah feel lik ah'm goan to cry.

He'd never been a big crier. He didn't have any practice *stopping.*

Whit's wrong wit mah face?

Catriona didn't seem to notice. She seemed annoyed and distracted.

"I've got news," she said. "I think Fiona is infected, after all. I think she's playing us."

Broch gasped. "Me *tae.*"

"You think *you're* infected?"

"Na, ah think *Fiona* is."

"Really? Why?"

Broch sat on the arm of the sofa and tried to look casual as he pushed the ring box into the cushions.

This wasn't the time. Catriona was distracted. Her mind wasn't on him or marriage.

He'd wait.

A great weight lifted from his shoulders as he returned to his Fiona story.

"Because Pete—"

He stopped.

Och.

He couldn't tell her he suspected Fiona had "inspired" Dr. Noseeum to steal his ring without letting her know about the ring.

"What about Pete?" prompted Catriona.

"He, uh—tell me aboot yours first. Ah interrupted ye."

She sighed. "Aaron, the studio head, bought an *evil* show— one I wouldn't have dreamt he'd bring to Parasol in a million years. I don't think it's a coincidence he's also been hanging out with Fiona."

"Mm," said Broch, nodding.

"Why do you think she's up to something?"

Broch's mind whirred.

"Em, Pete, uh, he said he was mean tae his *maw.*"

Catrina gaped. "His mom? He was mean to Joan? Wow. Those two are like peas in a pod."

Broch nodded. He'd dodged a bullet by spitting out a random mean thing. He hadn't even known if Pete's mom was *alive.*

"And he said he lashed out at his mom after he hung out with Fiona?"

"Aye. Yup."

Catriona grimaced. "So there you go. *Two* examples. We need to tell Anne. We need to reboot Fiona."

Broch glanced at the cushion where his ring sat tucked and stood.

"Aye. Let's git tae Anne's."

CHAPTER TEN

Fiona lay in bed.

She felt...*different.*

Her dalliance with Con had been a *fantastic* idea. The man was *incredible.* During their tryst, he'd done something to her—pulled energy from her somehow?—and while the process had left her feeling groggy, it had also been *immensely* pleasurable.

She smiled at the memory.

If this is how I die, I'm all in—

Her smile dropped.

Wait.

Rune absorbed people's energy. Is that what he'd been doing to his victims? Giving them death orgasms?

Her lip curled at the thought of it.

Ew.

No. Con's thing had to be different.

She wished her father had had the time to teach her the draining thing. She didn't love the idea of *eating* people, but if it made her look ten years younger? Or healed wounds?

Totally worth it.

And she didn't have to eat people *willy-nilly.* She could pick people who deserved it—men in jorts or improperly hemmed suit pants. Teenagers. Women with voices like hamsters.

All fair game.

But the weird feeling she had now was something *beyond* satisfying exhaustion. She found herself feeling...*warm and fuzzy?*

Happy? Open-hearted?

It was *weird.*

She needed to get up. Refocus.

Fiona took a shower to clear her head. As she towel-dried, her attention drew to her laptop, where it sat with its blinking blue light charging on her bedroom chair.

The list.

She still had the list of the other Kairos Joseph had been collecting. She suspected many of the people on it were normal humans wrapped up in some fantasy about being time travelers—*dorks*—but some of them had to be real.

She could connect with them. Use them as a base to build her brand following. Become Queen of the Nerds. It never hurt to have an army of adoring fans, no matter how weird they were.

Plus, if some *were* corrupted Kairos, maybe they could influence people to do things *for her.*

She smiled.

A lovely idea.

Discomfort bubbled in her chest like an unreleased burp.

On the other hand...

Her father was *crazy*, and it was wrong to manipulate those poor deluded people.

Wasn't it?

Ugh. She'd felt so sure she was on to something, and now she was confused again.

She *did* want the ability to reverse aging. That was key to her brand.

Renew, by Fiona.

Refresh, by Fiona.

Forever Young, by Fiona.

She'd have to work on the name later.

Was she going to have to ask Baby Rune for help?

Hm.

Maybe not.

Her father had mentioned another actress at the studio was helping him. What was her name?

Maddie.

Some DIY YouTube queen with a crafting show.

Maybe *she* knew something.

Fiona glanced at her watch.

No time to waste.

She had eleven interviews lined up in the next week, including one at two o'clock. Thanks to Rune kidnapping her, she was the hot story for this week's news cycle.

She couldn't go AWOL during her moment. She had to practice her teary storytelling. She had to decide which would play better; frightened and shaken or strong and defiant.

Defiant, I think.

That would play better for her brand. Today, she'd raise her profile as a strong woman. A survivor.

Maybe get an action-adventure franchise.

She'd be on every news outlet and every entertainment blog from Hollywood to Nova Scotia.

But first, she'd check out Maddie's. See if the woman knew anything about Rune's powers. Maybe *she* had powers.

If Maddie had her father's skills, Fiona could book her to teach her the ropes next week. By then, the Internet would have a new darling, and she'd have more time to devote to learning how to eat people.

Unless she got a book deal.

Then she'd have to work on that.

Hire a ghostwriter.

Blah, blah, blah...

CHAPTER ELEVEN

Broch and Catriona walked through Anne's amazing rental property to the patio, where Anne sat talking to Con.

"Jeffery let us in," said Catriona to announce their arrival. "But before we start training, we have some news."

"There's a lot of that going around," said Anne, throwing a side-eye at Con. "What's up?"

"We think Fiona's infected. She's got a friend of mine acting completely out of character, and the head of the studio—who she *is* or *was* dating—just bought a morally reprehensible show. It isn't like him."

Anne nodded but didn't say anything.

Not the response Catriona had expected.

"Should we make plans to siphon her?" she asked.

Anne shook her head. "We might need to keep her around for a little bit."

Catriona scowled. "Why?"

"As a hunting dog."

Con snorted a laugh. "God help you if she hears you call her a *dog*."

Catriona agreed. "You're not kidding. It made me nervous just *hearing* you say that."

Anne chuckled. "We have confirmation Fiona can sense other Kairos. We want her working for us in that capacity. It's a talent that could come in handy. It might help us figure out how widespread the problem is, too."

Catriona crossed her arms against her chest, considering the pros and cons of keeping her sister around as-is. "Great idea in theory, but anything you ask her to do, she'll run to do the opposite."

"We have a secret weapon." Anne motioned to Con.

"She's taken a shine to me," he said, grinning.

Catriona shrugged. "Okay. Good. Then you get to deal with her."

"Yes, we'll try Con's charms first," said Anne. She clapped her hands together. "In the meantime, let's figure out the best way to drain the bad guys."

Catriona nodded. She'd both been looking forward to training and dreading it. Now, the time was nigh.

Anne motioned to Broch. "You're going to be the bad guy."

He scowled. "But ah'm nae a bad guy."

"I know, but we need someone to beat up on."

"Och." He grinned. "Ah kin dae that."

"The key is we have to both be touching bare skin to siphon. The problem is, as soon as they feel themselves being drained, they're going to do everything possible to get away. It's a survival instinct for them at that point."

"Maybe some kind of head, arm, or leglock to keep them still?" suggested Catriona.

Anne nodded. "That's a good start. If one of us can get them in a lock, then the other will have time to join, and hopefully, we can make progress weakening them before they break free."

"Let's see," said Catriona, eyeing Broch. "An armbar would be good..."

Broch started lowering himself, and she shook her head.

"I don't think I'll be able to ask them to lay on their back, so you can't make it *too* easy for me."

Broch straightened.

She turned to Anne. "On the other hand, I can't exactly kick out Broch's knee."

Broch's eyes saucered. "Nae thank ye."

"If I get there first, I can pin them with my swords," suggested Anne. Orange light flared from her clenched fist, manifesting in the shape of an oversized dagger. She dropped to one knee to demonstrate, pressing the sword into the ground. "If I get them like this, they're pinned to the ground or the wall or wherever—like a bug. But we need multiple options, especially if you get to them first."

"Yeah, I don't have any magic swords," agreed Catriona.

Anne chewed her bottom lip. "I was thinking about this last night, and I had a crazy thought if you want to give it a try."

"I'm game."

"Since I'm faster than you, I was trying to think of a way to speed you up."

Catriona frowned. "You're making me feel like a loser."

Anne chuckled. "What do you think about me throwing you into him?"

"*Throwing* me?"

"I'm thinking it might kill two birds with one stone. I throw you into him, he's knocked down, you hold him and then I join."

Catriona nodded. "Um, I'm still having trouble picturing the whole *I throw you into him* part."

Anne shrugged. "Let's give it a shot. Broch, you stand over there." She motioned into the grassy area beside the pool, and he took his place there.

Catriona moved to stand next to Anne.

"Try and relax at the beginning of this," said Anne.

"Riiight. That should be easy—*whoop!*"

Before Catriona could finish her sentence, Anne grabbed her wrist with one hand, dipped to grab her ankle with the other, and then spun her like a two-year-old getting helicopter rides from her father.

Catriona only had one thought.

I am going to die.

After a few revolutions, Anne flung her at Broch. Like a bullet launched from a gun, Catriona found herself flying through the air with no ability to maneuver or stop. She lifted her arms to protect herself as her imminent crash into Broch approached. She winced, bracing. The moment of impact came...and went.

Huh?

Catriona opened her eyes, baffled as to why she hadn't slammed into Broch. Instead, it felt as if a squid tentacle had wrapped around her waist and snatched her from the air.

She found herself cradled in Broch's arms like a baby. He smiled down at her.

"You stepped out of the way," scolded Anne.

Broch nodded. "Aye. She was goan tae crash intae me."

"That was the *point*. She's supposed to knock you over and put you in an arm lock."

"Bit she'd be hurt."

Anne sighed. "Let's try it again. This time, let her knock

you over."

Broch released Catriona's legs to the ground. "Bit she willnae."

Anne cocked her head. "Are you suggesting I *can't* knock you over with her?"

"Hold on, hold on," said Catriona. "I'm a *person* here, you know, not a bowling ball. Don't start flinging me at each other."

Anne put her hands on her hips. "Broch, what I'm saying is *let* yourself be knocked over. And Catriona, you put him in a lock as soon as possible."

"So we're *really* going to do this again?" Catriona slumped back toward Anne, feeling uneasy about her chances of surviving training.

She took her place beside the redhead and clenched her teeth.

"Ready?' asked Anne.

"*No*. But I never—*Whoop!*"

Anne jerked her up again, spun her twice, and flung her at Broch. Feeling slightly more prepared this time, Catriona braced herself for the hit. Once again, Broch sidestepped and caught her, bringing her to a gentle halt, flipping her, and cradling her in his arms.

She smiled up at him. "This isn't so bad, after all."

"*Broch!*" Anne sounded exasperated.

The highlander shrugged. "Ah cannae help it. Ah cannae let her get hurt."

"You mean it's physically impossible for you *not* to protect her?"

Broch nodded. "Ah ken sae."

Anne nodded. "You moved much faster than a normal human. You'd have to in order to catch her the way you did. I'm thinking you might have powers activated by protecting her."

He shrugged again and smiled down at Catriona, who remained dangling in his arms like a bolt of fabric.

"It's whit ah dae," he said.

She grinned.

"I'm okay with that."

CHAPTER TWELVE

Fiona rapped on Maddie's door and glanced at her watch for the hundredth time. She was cutting it close. It had taken her an hour to hunt down the actress' address and get to her place. Kiki, Aaron's receptionist, had refused to give Maddie's information to her.

Kiki didn't like her much.

Thank goodness she'd thought to steal every bit of info she could find on Aaron's computer during her time with him. The old creep had fallen asleep with her still in his house. That was back when she'd been *securing her position* for a move from her old studio to the larger and more prestigious Parasol Pictures.

She couldn't *not* take advantage of the situation. Sometimes, a little blackmail came in handy. Information was *king.*

She'd been hoping to catch the DIY craft show actress on the Parasol lot, but she couldn't find anyone who'd seen her in a couple of days. A car Fiona assumed to be Maddie's sat in the woman's driveway, though, so things were looking up. Maybe she was sick.

She'd corner Maddie, find out if she had Rune's powers or if she knew how his worked, and then be off in plenty of time to get to her two o'clock interview.

"Maddie?" she called out, knocking again, a little louder this time. She rested her hand on the doorknob and gave it a turn, expecting little.

It gave.

Maddie left her door unlocked?

She looked down the street.

In this neighborhood?

She pushed open the door and poked her head inside. The drapes were drawn. The living room was dark and quiet.

"Maddie?"

Nothing.

She tiptoed toward the back of the house. The first room off the hall, a guest bedroom, was empty but for a pile of clothes Fiona wouldn't wear on a bet. They were spread across a bed as if someone had been pulling things for Goodwill or...ugh—*packing*?

Was Maddie planning on wearing that dress with the polka dots and lace in *public*? Was she filling in for Minnie Mouse at Disneyland?

Fiona continued to the master bedroom and peeked inside. It, too, was empty. The white sheets of an unmade bed glowed back at her.

Looking for the en suite bath, she opened the door to instead find a shallow closet. Confused, she made a full rotation, searching for another door.

No en suite?

She walked to the hallway.

Does she use the hall bathroom?

Fiona shook her head.

The woman lives like an *animal*.

Fiona retraced her steps to the living room. Maybe Maddie had been nothing more than her father's girlfriend, after all.

Wouldn't that be tragic?

It meant her father—arguably one of the most powerful beings on the planet—had been sleeping with a woman who was nothing more than a glorified *social media influencer*.

Gross.

She was about to leave when she noticed a pile of something on the floor.

A rounded pyramid of...*ash*?

Fiona bent lower and lower as she approached the pile.

What is that?

She poked her finger into the side of the lump, and her nail sunk in, flecks from the top raining to either side of her digit-like curtains.

Dust?

It looked as if someone had dumped out a vacuum. Maybe ash from a fireplace? But there was no fire—

Hold on.

Wait a second.

The sliding dust revealed a gold chain. Fiona lifted it from the pile to find a tiny hammer dangling from it.

Something a DIY queen might wear.

Uh oh.

Didn't her father say the people he drained turned to dust? *Poof?*

She refocused on the pile.

Maddie?

Had her father *eaten* Maddie?

He'd been there when he was still an adult. He'd made it as far as Maddie's house. Why hadn't he stayed there? Maddie's would have been a great place to hide. Instead, he'd left and ended up being rebooted by the Goody-Two-Shoes Squad.

Maybe Maddie threatened to turn him in?

Good reason to eat her.

Or maybe he was just hungry. Or injured. He could have snapped. Who knew? Long story short, Maddie screwed up and got dusted, and then her father screwed up and left to be captured by Catriona and the angels.

Fiona cocked her head.

Catriona and the Angels.

Sounds like a band.

She dropped the chain and dusted her hands. She wiped them on the sofa.

Ew.

She took a step toward the front door and then stopped.

She turned to stare at the pile.

What would happen when Maddie didn't show up for work?

Eventually, someone would come to her house and find the ashes. Maybe they'd test them and figure out they used to be Maddie.

They wouldn't know what to make of it. There'd be spontaneous combustion rumors in the gossip rags. Maybe they'd think some deranged killer was cremating people and leaving their ashes behind. But Fiona didn't want the authorities on the *lookout* for piles of ash before she figured out how to drain people. She didn't plan to suck people to ash—more like *borrow* a little life from them—but she might need practice, and accidents happened...

If someone had seen her come into Maddie's house and

then she was spotted *again* in the vicinity of *another* pile in the future—that would be bad.

Best to clean up Maddie.

She moved back down the hallway to open a closet door.

Bingo.

Vacuum.

She pulled out the old Dirt Devil and plugged it in before taking a good five minutes to figure out how it worked.

It had been a *long* time since she'd cleaned her own house.

When the red monster roared to life, she inched it towards the dust pile and watched the flecks suck into it, disappearing like a desert sand storm sweeping over the horizon.

I'll cover your tracks, Dad.

Looks like she'd have to work with Baby Rune after all. He could teach her how to reverse time and trauma, and she'd teach him how the police worked. That info could come in handy for a guy who left dead people everywhere he went.

She'd been a minor character on enough cop shows to be quite the expert.

She sucked up the rest of Maddie and tucked her back in the closet.

Closing the door, she paused.

No.

She couldn't leave a bag of human ash for the cops to find. If they thought there'd been foul play, they might look at the contents of the vacuum. She'd end up on *Dateline* with everyone going, "Why'd the idiot leave Maddie in the closet for the cops to find?"

With a huff, she hauled out the vacuum again. Turning it on seemed like a *dream* next to figuring out how to get the bag out of it. When she finally did unhook it, she replaced it with another bag from the shelf in the closet and put it away.

Thank you, Maddie, for being prepared with spare bags.

She wiped down everything she'd touched with a dish towel, took the towel and her dusty, disgusting trophy, and left.

She drove miles out of her way and stopped along the side of the road to release Maddie to the desert winds. As she tore the bag, the wind shifted, blowing half the dead woman onto her clothes.

And into her *hair*.

Fiona fought hard not to retch.

Gag reflex squelched, she undressed to her underwear, shook out her hair, and left the vacuum bag there as a makeshift grave marker.

It didn't serve its purpose for long. A breeze caught the bag, and it tumbled down the road as she pulled a change of clothes from her trunk. She kept clothes handy in case the paparazzi showed up, and she needed to look *fresh*.

Changed and ash-free, she headed back to Hollywood to get to her interview.

She'd be late.

After that, she'd find Baby Daddy.

CHAPTER THIRTEEN

A policeman stopped Sean as he walked toward the gates of the Bel Air mansion. Several police cruisers sat outside the estate, lights flashing. A small crowd had gathered across the residential street, craning their necks for a better view.

Sean had told police officer Dennis Hartmann—and most of the rest of the LAPD at one point or another—to give him a call if anyone involved with Parasol Pictures ever showed up on their radar. Drunk driving, domestic issues, drunk and disorderly, drugs, parking tickets—it didn't matter. If a Parasol asset was in trouble, he needed to know as soon as possible so they could get ahead of the press.

He'd gotten a call.

"I'm looking for Officer Dennis Hartmann," said Sean.

The officer at the mansion's gate asked him to wait. He directed another officer standing nearby to fetch Dennis.

A minute later, Dennis appeared on the home's stoop and called to his fellow officer.

"He's cool. Let him in."

The gate cop allowed Sean access. He walked straight to Dennis.

"How are you doing?" he asked, reaching to shake the man's hand.

"Good, Sean, how about you?"

"Great. You have something for me?"

"Yeah..." Dennis scratched the back of his head and chuckled. "I gotta tell you—when you told me to keep an eye out, I figured my first call would be about a domestic—but not like this."

Sean looked up at the large home. "I'm not familiar with this place. Whose is it?"

"Huck Carter. Follow me, but watch your step."

Sean followed Dennis inside. Crime techs were busy at work, and Dennis kept Sean from entering the living room of the open-plan home. Dennis motioned to what looked like a mound of ash laying between a coffee table and a chair. The gray pile stood out against the white furniture and rugs. A man stood over it, taking photos.

"There it is," said Dennis.

Sean scowled. "What is it?"

"Ash. Huck's got a missing wife and kid, and that was left behind. You think it's a calling card?"

Sean recalled Anne mentioning the Angeli had come to investigate in the first place because someone—who they now knew was Rune—had been draining humans, leaving behind ash. But Rune was in Angeli jail. This pile meant Rune wasn't the only sick Kairos with draining powers.

Great.

Sean's attention dropped to a collection of framed photos sitting on top of a grand piano to his right. He picked up a portrait of a couple. The wife held a baby in her arms.

"Where's Huck now?" he asked.

"Down at the station. He says he doesn't know anything. Says he was at work, came home, found the place empty and the pile there. No ransom note, no calls—we've got nothing. He figured she was out shopping, but it's been hours." He jerked a thumb in the direction of the garage. "Plus, her car's here."

Sean scanned the other photos, finding the same repeated vignettes—husband, wife, boy—the boy in various stages of development. The kid looked about five in what he assumed was the most recent photo.

Sean was about to head outside when he noticed several drawings hanging from the large custom-paneled refrigerator.

"Mind if I take a step in there?" he asked, motioning to the kitchen.

Dennis shook his head. "Nah. Make it quick though."

Sean entered the kitchen to stare at the drawings. The one that had caught his eye had one word on it, written in thick letters in black crayon. What looked like fire and lightning burst from the edges of the letters, scribbled in red, orange, and yellow.

He pulled out his phone and took a picture of it.

"Got a thing for kids' art?" asked Dennis.

Sean made sure he had the photo and then turned to the officer.

"Is this the kid's name?"

"Kid's name is Oliver," said Dennis, returning his attention to the drawing to read the black letters there. "Why would you think the kid's name is *Rune*?"

CHAPTER FOURTEEN

Fiona entered the lobby of her building and walked to the gray-haired attendant stationed behind the desk.

"Teddy, can you get my car washed?" she asked.

It wouldn't hurt to get the car swept for any traces of Maddie.

"Sure, Miss Fiona." He nodded toward the lobby behind her. "You have a visitor waiting for you."

Teddy didn't need to tell her. She'd felt the presence a moment before he spoke. Someone like her. A *Kairos*, as the Angel Michael liked to call them.

She turned to find a pre-teen boy sitting in a large leather chair, staring at the ground.

She expelled a breath.

Whew.

Not Rune.

A tiny, sick part of her felt disappointed. She needed to talk to Rune if she was ever going to crack his powers. Plus, she wanted to tell Rune she'd cleaned up Maddie for him. Maybe get a pat on the back for a job well done.

Why did she still want to impress him?

She sighed. More fodder for her therapist.

Anyway, this wasn't Rune. Rune was a little guy, but this random teen was someone *like* Rune. She could feel that. Maybe one of Rune's nutty followers—one of the people from the list she'd stolen from Joseph?

Oh no...

If those whackjobs had found a way to track *her* down at home...

Not good.

She took a step toward the boy.

"Can I help you?" she asked, tensing, preparing to run if he pulled a weapon or leaped at her.

He glared at her through eyes so blue they appeared almost white.

Shit.

"Yes, you can help me, daughter," said Rune.

She glanced back at Teddy. The old man had wandered off.

Good.

She didn't need strangers overhearing teenage boys call her *daughter.* It would end up in some tabloid about her obsession with underage kinky sex games or something. Even old Teddy wasn't above spreading trashy gossip if the price was right.

She hustled to sit in a chair across from the boy, perched on the edge so she could run should the need present itself. She needed to question him fast—before Teddy came back. She needed to find out what was going on, and she had *no* intention of inviting him to her apartment. The last time Rune was alone with her, she'd had to stab him in the neck with a pen and run away—him screaming, bleeding, and lumbering after her like some kind of meth-head zombie.

She pinched together her index finger and thumb. "You were tiny—?"

"I'm correcting my mistake," he said. "Energy not only heals—it helps me become my perfect self."

Fiona nodded.

Clear as mud.

Teddy shuffled back into the room, and she flashed him a nervous smile. He eyed the boy and pretended to fuss with something on his desk.

Dammit.

She raised her hand to cover her mouth from his view.

"When you say *energy*, do you mean you're *eating* people again?" she whispered to Rune.

He nodded. "I need a couple more. I think twenty-five would be a perfect age. What do you think? Maybe older to be sure my minions respect me?"

He eyed Teddy.

"*No*," snapped Fiona guessing his intentions.

Rune looked dismayed. "But he's right *there*..."

"*No.* You don't shit where you eat."

"What does that mean?"

She shook her head. "How can you be so *old* and still know nothing about human habits, or speech, or pop culture—"

"Because I am focused on my *mission*," he answered with as much gravitas as his pubescent voice could offer.

She sighed. "It means don't bring trouble where you live—or in this case, where *I* live. Get it? Teddy's not a snack."

"Did you need something?" asked Teddy, overhearing his name.

Clearly, he was straining to eavesdrop.

Fiona raised a hand and smiled. "No, Teddy. We're good."

I just saved you from being sucked into ash. Consider that your Christmas bonus.

Rune slapped his hands against his thighs. "Well, I wanted to stop by and let you know I don't need your help getting on the studio lot, but I will need you to help me locate and lead my followers. I can't be bothered with the day-to-day. You'll do."

Fiona scowled. The last thing she wanted to be was her father's lackey.

"I don't—wait, what do you mean you don't need my help getting onto the studio lot?"

"My father in my current reincarnation works there."

"Your *father*? Who?"

"Huck Carter."

"Huck—?" Her jaw dropped. "Your *father* is *Huck Carter*?"

Fiona was stunned. That explained *a lot*. She wasn't in danger of winning any philanthropic awards, but even she found Huck's show evil. Now, it made sense. The poor schmuck had been living with Rune. It was like having a tumor that ate every good impulse.

Speaking of Huck…

She motioned to Rune. "Isn't Huck going to find your growth spurt disconcerting?"

Rune shrugged. "No. He'll do what I say."

Fiona nodded. *Now* seemed like a bad time to bring up her desire to learn how to suck the fountain of youth from people. Rune looked hungry.

She was a little afraid he'd show her by eating *her*.

"Great," she said instead. "I'll see you later—"

"I need Joseph's list. You have it," he said, lowering his icy gaze to her.

Fiona felt her blood run cold.

"Hm?"

"You have Joseph's list. I know you do."

Fiona rubbed her face with her hands. She used to love that Rune favored her over Catriona. Whenever she mentioned her sister, he acted as if he'd never even heard of her. It was *crazy*. It used to make her feel special.

Now, she was starting to wonder if Catriona had gotten the better end of the deal.

As much as some sick part of her still wanted to impress him, she wasn't ready to give him the list. The list was her last bargaining chip with Team Highlander should they set their sights on rebooting her.

She shrugged. "Seriously, I don't know what you're talking about."

Rune's skinny arm snapped out like a whip. His fingers locked on her wrist, and he squeezed it as he spoke.

"I'm going to go eat, and then you and I will take that list and—"

"There you are," said Con, bursting through the front door of the apartment building with boundless boyish energy. "I've been looking—*holy blessed Mother Mary*."

As he swore and recoiled, Fiona realized the Irishman had seen Rune's freaky eyes.

"Hey, *Rune*," said Fiona, steadily tugging at her father's grip on her wrist. "Do you remember Con? He's a Sentinel like the one who destroyed Joseph."

Rune's demeanor changed. His grip on her wrist loosened. She saw his ego wrestling against the reasonable assumption that he should avoid engaging Con in his bird-boned teenage body.

"Con's even more powerful, though," she added in the hopes of pushing Rune's decision even further in favor of self-preservation.

Her father released her and stood. Fiona scrambled away, as casually as possible, to stand near Con.

"I'll be back," said Rune. He skirted around the Irishman, staying as far away from him as he could while still beelining for the exit. Outside, he pulled up the hood of his sweat jacket and strode away, looking like any moody kid.

"That was yer da?" asked Con, watching him go. "I thought the Angels had him?"

Fiona grimaced. She didn't want to tell Con anything. She needed time to think.

"Should I go after him, or do I need Catriona?" he asked.

He waited for an answer. When none came, he leaned close and whispered in her ear, his warm breath giving her happy shivers.

"Ye want to go upstairs for a bit instead?" he asked.

She nodded.

"Yes, please."

CHAPTER FIFTEEN

Huck walked through the police station parking lot, fishing in his pockets for the keys to his SUV. The conversation he'd had with the police ran in a loop through his head.

He felt *guilty*. He didn't know why. He didn't know anything about his wife and child's disappearance, and he'd told them as much. It was the truth.

Maybe he felt bad because he didn't *care* that his wife had gone missing? He'd been trying to find a graceful way to shake her for *years*.

Maybe it wasn't *guilt*. Maybe it was the fear they'd sense his apathy and consider him a suspect.

It was always the spouse, after all.

He *was* concerned about the boy, though...not wildly so.

Oliver was weird.

The kid had been creeping him out since day one, what with those crazy light blue eyes and his strange sullen ways. He suspected the kid wasn't his. Told his wife as much. He'd never gotten around to getting the DNA test but those *eyes*... Both he and his wife had brown eyes.

Maybe Ashley ran away and took the kid with her. That would be fine. She *would* hide if she ran away. She knew he had friends and followers who would make her life a living hell if she came after him or he decided to come after her.

He chuckled to himself.

Wherever she was, she wouldn't have to hide very hard.

He had *no* intention of looking for her, and he could make a new, better son with a new, better wife.

A kid without those freaky eyes.

He didn't wish the child *harm*, but he didn't want him back *without* his wife. If only Oliver came back, he'd have to take care of him on his own.

Nightmare.

He imagined that's why boarding schools existed.

If Ashley was gone, he could play the grieving husband and never have to pay child support. Win-win. The tragic story would give him a huge rating boost. He could stay at the top of the news cycles for *weeks*. Women would be falling over themselves to console him. He already had two interns who practically dropped their panties every time he walked into a room.

He wasn't a runway model by any stretch. He wasn't deluded enough to think he was. Ashley, in a pique of anger, once told him he looked like a ferret in a wig. Didn't matter. Money and power made up for all that when it came to the ladies.

Worked on her, didn't it?

Ashley had been a perfect wife in the beginning. Then she got all these ideas in her head and—*ugh.*

Worst-case scenario—they really were kidnapped, and she came back childless. He'd have to wait a year before he divorced her to keep from looking like a monster.

Or not. Nobody cared in the end. He could claim he suspected *she* killed the child. *Whatever.* His followers understood what a drain a grieving wife could be.

Huck found his keys and looked up to see a boy about twelve or thirteen-years-old leaning against his black Escalade.

"Hey, get away from there," he snapped.

Kids had no appreciation for how hard it was to keep a shine on a vehicle.

"We don't have much time," said the urchin.

"Time? Look, you little—"

Huck stopped in his tracks.

The boy stared at him with ice-blue eyes.

Nerves danced in Huck's stomach.

"Who are you?" he asked.

His mind raced in pursuit of answers. Maybe this was Oliver's brother? Maybe Oliver's true father was near?

"It's me. *Rune*," said the boy.

Huck echoed the word.

"Rune?"

Rune was the stupid nickname his son insisted on being called. How did this kid know about it? Or did all kids want to be called Rune now? Was it code? Some kind of social media challenge? Could he build a show around it?

The boy stretched his neck until it cracked. "I have some things to take care of, but I'll be back for you. Get ready. We need to start the war."

Huck shifted from annoyed to *pissed*. He didn't know who this little idiot was, but the kid hadn't bothered to do his homework.

He sneered. "If you're pretending to be my son, he's *six*, moron."

The kid took a step forward.

Nothing about him felt human.

Fear made Huck sweat.

This was no *kid*.

"Do you have Oliver?" he asked.

"I *am* Rune. I told you that." The boy's nose wrinkled as if he'd smelled something rancid. "You know I'm not *your* kid. You've always known. I could tell. Even before my memories returned."

"Where's Ashley?"

"I used mother's energy to age. I didn't know if it would work, but you can see it did." He smiled with what looked like pride and then mumbled, "I'll need a few more like her."

Huck felt like he was doing a puzzle where every other piece had been swapped out with one from a different set.

"You need a few more *what*?"

Rune held up a hand. "Stop. I'm going to need you to get me on the Parasol Pictures lot and help me reach my followers."

Huck scowled and attempted to appear angry. He *was* angry—he was just a lot more scared than pissed. He didn't want to appear as frightened as he felt. Weakness was always a bad look.

Part of him also wanted to smack this brat into next week.

Time to lay down the rules.

"Look, I don't know who you think you are—"

"I think I am your lord and master. I think you're *lucky* I need you, or you'd be a pile of ash sitting next to your wife's."

Huck opened his mouth, but words failed him.

What am I supposed to say to that?

Wait.

An odd thought occurred to him.

Did the kid turn Ashley into a pile of ash *because* her name was *Ash*ley? If her name had been Peggy, would she have fallen into a pile of wooden dowels?

"Is it because her name is Ashley?" he asked.

Rune's brow knit. "What?"

"If her name was Lily—"

Huck slapped his hand over his mouth.

What is wrong with me?

He had to be in shock or something to be stuck on such a stupid train of thought. His brain was trying to avoid the rest of the nonsense.

Before Huck could form a sentence, the boy continued.

"I didn't travel through time to chit-chat with you. I didn't perfect rebirth to lose this moment. I came *here* for a reason. I chose *you* for a reason."

Huck squinted at him.

"Did you say *rebirth*?"

Another dumb question, but at least he didn't ask what would have happened if Ashley's name was Ruby.

That would have been pretty cool, actually.

Rune waggled a closed fist at Huck, his thumb pointed skyward like a politician delivering a speech. "The key is *concentrating.* If you feel death or a healing hop coming on, you think *hard* about where you want to be—time *and* place—and then you—"

Huck's mind hadn't finished processing the first part of Rune's confessions. He had *no* idea what the kid was talking about now. He wasn't sure this part was even in English.

The boy stopped as if he sensed his words were going to waste. As he paused to flash his disapproval, Huck realized he'd missed an opportunity to learn more about the strange creature in front of him.

Too late.

Rune pulled a burner phone from the pocket of his baggy jeans and handed it to Huck.

"I've found these come in handy in this time. Take the number."

Huck did as he was told. He wasn't sure why. When he had the burner number on his phone, he handed it back.

Rune slid the phone back into his pocket. "I'll be back. I

need to find Fiona."

"Fiona?"

"My daughter."

"Your *daughter*?"

Rune scowled. "Why do you keep repeating everything I say?"

Huck shook his head. The name Fiona rang a bell.

"Fiona who? *Duffy*?"

"Who?"

"Is your daughter Fiona *Duffy*? The actress? Dark hair? Works for Parasol?"

Rune pursed his lips in a haughty way kids just didn't do. "She is often on the Parasol Pictures lot," he confirmed.

"Fiona Duffy..." Huck clucked his tongue. "Who else is related—?"

Rune waved him away. "Ashley isn't coming back. Do what you have to do to get the authorities out of our lives. I'll leave that part up to you."

The boy walked away without haste or another word.

Huck watched him go until he found the will to shut his gaping maw.

Did he say 'travel through time'?

CHAPTER SIXTEEN

Con watched as Fiona guzzled water and tried to talk at the same time. For a woman who'd been playing coy in the lobby when he arrived, now he couldn't get her to shut up.

He'd found himself a perch on her sofa, but not before jogging from her bed to her bathroom to punch a hole through her shower tiles. It was the only way he could think of to release the *darkness* writhing in him. Every time he made love to Fiona, he felt overwhelmed with anger. After round two, there was *no* doubt in his mind their trysts somehow cleansed her and sullied him. Every time he sipped her energy, she became happier and lighter, and he longed to lay whole cities to waste.

Luckily for nearby cities, he seemed able to work through his jolt of evil and keep it at bay until it passed.

Less lucky for the bathroom tiles.

He didn't know if Fiona was *cursed*, but after everything he'd seen in his life, it wouldn't surprise him. Angels. Hundred-year-old pirate queens. *He'd* been a ghost for a while, and he'd *met* another ghost...

Why not witches?

Maybe he could use a witch's curse to *silence* her. With her load lightened, Fiona was blabbering away like she'd mainlined a pot of espresso.

She lowered her bottle of water. "And then—you saw him—the second time Rune's almost a *teenager*. Then, he says he's going to use *his* dad from this reincarnation to get onto the Parasol lot, and his dad is *Huck Carter*. Can you believe it?"

"Wow." Con shook his head. He had no idea who Huck Carter was.

Fiona drank some more. Water ran in rivulets on both sides

of her mouth, creating twin rivers flanking her chin and throat before disappearing somewhere between her breasts, which sat beneath an oversized men's tee shirt.

Not *his*.

Luckily, he wasn't a jealous man. Though, having so recently absorbed his shot of evil from Fiona, he *was* having some nasty thoughts...

"Whose shirt is that?" he asked.

She glanced down at it. "This old thing? No idea."

He grunted.

In his mind, he ran through what she'd told him so far. It might be better for him to concentrate on the information she was sharing before he started looking through her phone for men to beat up.

"So, *em*...who's this *Maddie* person again? Yer sure it was her? The dust?" he asked. She'd told him someone was dead—reduced to a pile of ash—and then hadn't paused a second before moving on.

He thought it might be something important.

Fiona put down the bottle and wiped her mouth on the back of her arm. "Pretty sure. Rune does that to people, you know. Sucks them dry and uses their energy to heal."

"And you think he did that to this Maddie person?"

"Yes." She glanced at the door. "I suppose you could test the vacuum for DNA..."

"The vacuum?"

"I sucked her up and dumped her in the desert. The bag is there somewhere, too, blowing around. We could probably find it if we had to."

"Riiight..."

Her attention drifted. "What do you think of cats? I was thinking about getting a cat..." Her gaze bounced back to him. "I think the little monster ate his *mom*. It's how he's growing up so fast. Do you think I need Botox here?" She pointed to her forehead.

"No." Con realized Fiona's manic phase was the perfect time to talk her into working for them.

"Hey, how'd you like a job?" he asked.

She scowled. "An acting job?"

"No. Better. A *spy* job."

"You want me to spy on Rune?"

"No. Well, yes, that would be good too, but we were thinking—"

"Who's we?"

"Em, me and, er, Annie and *Michael*..." He emphasized Michael's name, and Fiona lit up like a barber's pole.

He *knew* he'd been her second choice.

Begorra, I hate that bastard.

He continued. "We were thinking ye could help us identify sick Kairos. 'Cuz you can do that sort of thing. Yer amazin'.'"

He smiled. *Might as well butter her up.*

She smiled back at him.

That's probably a good sign...

"Would I be working directly with Michael?" she asked, trying to look nonchalant and failing miserably.

She wasn't a very good actress, as it turned out.

"Aye," he said. "*Very* close."

Next time I see that Angel, I'm goin' to beat the livin' shite out of him...

"You   said   he   can   do   that   thing   you   do? she asked. "The, uh..."

"The pleasure thing. Aye." He almost added *even better than me,* but at this point, his ego could only take so much.

She nodded. "Sure. I'd love to help."

"Great, I'll let them—er, *Michael*—know."

"Okay." She held out the water. Only a spit remained at the bottom. "Do you want some?"

"No, thank ye, luv. So, em, how does yer teenage father want ye to help him? Did he say?"

She burped and patted her chest. "He wants the list."

"What list?"

"The—" Fiona's eyes grew wide, and she slapped the hand not holding the bottle over her mouth.

"What have you done to me?" she mumbled from behind her fingers.

"What are ye fussin' about?"

"Did you drug me?"

Con chuckled. "*No*, why would I drug you?"

"I don't know..." She motioned to his crotch. "Did you put it on your—"

"You think I put some kind of poison on my—" He covered his crotch with his hands. "*Are ye mad*?"

"Sorry." She scowled and wiped her forehead. "Is it hot in

here?"

CHAPTER SEVENTEEN

Catriona lay on the lounge chair by the pool, panting and sweating from her training session with Anne. Once they realized Broch was no help because he couldn't stop trying to save her, she continued working with Anne, and the big Highlander had toddled off for a lesson in mixology from Jeffrey. The two of them had been laughing and drinking for the last three hours while she was wheezing and getting bested at every turn by a semi-immortal pirate queen.

Life isn't fair.

She'd considered herself a good fighter, but Anne, with her enhanced strength, speed, and flexibility, was *next level.* She'd learned some new moves, and together they'd choreographed some takedowns for imaginary foes of various sizes and skill levels.

Later, she'd be grateful. Right now, she was exhausted.

Her phone rang, and she groaned as she reached for where it sat on the glass table beside her, certain her arm would soon be decorated with bruises.

It was Sean.

"Hey," she answered.

"We've got a situation," said Sean.

She snorted a laugh. "When don't we?"

"Rune is loose."

Catriona sat up. "What? Where? How do you know?"

"I got a call from a cop. He's got a missing wife, a missing six-year-old kid, and a pile of ash."

"Why would you assume the pile of ash is from Rune? Maybe there's another one like him?"

"The boy's name is Oliver, but word is he insisted on being

called *Rune*. There are child's drawings all over the refrigerator with that word."

Catriona let out a breath. "You're kidding me."

"Nope. That, and a pile of ash where his mom used to be...pretty damning evidence."

"You said this is a Parasol asset? Who?"

"Huck Carter."

Catriona gasped. "Is he missing, too?"

"No. He's alive and well."

"Like a cockroach." The phrase *only the good die young* ran through Catriona's head.

She had so many questions.

"Why would Rune come back here as a *kid*? If he wanted to return for revenge, you'd think he'd want to be a grown-up to do it?"

"You'd think," agreed Sean.

"And how did he get away from the Angeli? Did they kill him?" She sucked in a breath. "Did we forget to tell them not to kill him?"

Sean clucked his tongue. "I have a theory. I don't know how he died, but I think he screwed up and undershot the year to be reborn."

"I need to tell Anne. Maybe she can get more info from Michael about how this happened."

"That's why I called. Tell her Rune is on the loose like some real-life Chucky doll."

She chuckled. "At least he's a kid. I assume that will make it easier to siphon him."

"Hopefully."

"Anne's got a plan to use Fiona as a bloodhound. Maybe we can get her to find him."

Sean scoffed. "That plan seems doomed from the start."

"Could be. I'll give you a call if we hear anything."

"Ditto."

Catriona hung up to find Anne staring at her.

"What's up?" she asked.

Catriona flopped back on her lounge chair because it took too much effort to remain sitting up. "That was Sean. That guy I told you about with the terrible television show? His wife has been drained to a pile of dust, and we think his son is Rune, reborn."

Anne gaped. "*Rune*? How can that be?"

Catriona shrugged. "You might want to give Michael a call."

Anne's jaw clenched. "I knew he was acting weird. I'm going to..."

Anne faded off as she stormed inside, nearly knocking over Jeffrey as he weaved his way to the patio following his day of drinking with Broch.

Broch, who'd been swimming to clear his head of Jeffrey's fancy cocktails, stepped out of the pool looking like a sea god as usual.

Jeffrey eyed him. "I will never get tired of that," he mumbled. He turned his attention to Catriona. "This might be the best day of my life. He's delightful. Can I keep him?"

"You're welcome to try," said Catriona, tittering.

Jeffrey gasped. "Oh, I almost forgot why I came out here. Your sister's here."

Catriona's smile evaporated. "She is?"

Jeffrey nodded. "Upstairs. With Con."

"Upstairs—?"

"In a *bedroom*," drawled Jeffrey. "It sounds like baboons fighting."

Catriona winced "Oh, *gross*. I am *so* sorry."

As if invoked, Con appeared on the patio looking like a man on a mission. He stormed forward and, without a second of hesitation, wrapped his arms around Jeffrey, hoisted him up, and dropped him into the pool.

"*Hey*," roared Broch after watching the moment unfold. "Why dinnae ye pick on someone closer tae yer size?"

Jeffrey sputtered to the surface. "Kill him, Broch. *Please*. Do us all a favor."

"Aye. Hit me," said Con, raising his fists.

Broch scowled. "Whit?"

"*Hit me*, ye great Scottish oaf." Con took a swing at him, and Broch dodged.

Broch looked at Catriona. "Whit is wrong wit—"

Before he could finish, Con dove at his midsection and Broch fell into the pool with the Irishman on top of him.

Jeffrey hustled out of the water.

"Oh, my God. That was like being trapped in a tank with a squid and whale," he said, scurrying to Catriona's side.

The two men found their feet in the shallow end, their upper halves rising from the water as they exchanged blows.

"Stop it!" yelled Catriona.

"Mm. Stop it. No," drawled Jeffrey, his eyes locked on the battle. Broch smacked Con across the face with a strong blow.

Jeffrey applauded and cheered.

"Go, Highlander!"

Catriona moved to the edge of the pool. "Broch, don't hurt him."

Con crushed his fist into the side of Broch's face. Broch stumbled back and looked at Catriona.

"Hurt *him*?"

Anne stormed from the house.

"Cut it out! Right now!" she barked, her orange sword extending from her right fist.

Having been separated by Con's last blow, the men stood in the water, panting.

"Aye. I think I'm good now," said Con.

Anne retracted her blade. "What the hell is going on?"

Con ran his hand over his head to slide his bedraggled locks back into place. "It's the darkness. From Fiona. I have to find a way to expend it."

Catriona caught Anne's eyes.

"He and Fiona were upstairs," she explained.

Anne scowled. "*Ew.*"

Catriona nodded. "That's what I said."

Con put his hands on his hips and looked exasperated. "I'm pullin' the evil out of her. It's a *job*."

Anne's attention shifted to Jeffery, who stood fully clothed and dripping by the chairs. "What happened to *you*?"

"Con threw me in the pool."

Anne's eyebrows arched. "That wasn't nice."

"That's the *point*," said Con. He extended a hand and waded a step closer to Broch. "I'm sorry, *boyo*. I thought it best to finish with ye. I would've killed Jeffrey. He's made of paper and chintz."

Jeffrey scowled. "God, I hate him."

Broch shook Con's hand and felt his jaw. "Nice richt."

"Thanks. You too." Con's eye had swollen shut. He transformed into crackling maroon light and then reappeared beside Anne, dry and unharmed.

"That's nae fair," said Broch, wading out of the pool.

Anne sighed. "Hopefully, this was all worth it because we

need Fiona to find Rune."

"We were just talking to him," said Con.

Anne and Catriona's attention shot to him.

"Who? *Rune*?" they asked in stereo.

Con nodded. "He went to Fiona's to talk to her. That's why I'm here—to tell you."

"Why didn't you grab him?" asked Anne.

"Sean said he's six years old," added Catriona. "You could have snatched him up and brought him to us."

Con shook his head. "Not the Rune I saw. He was a teenager."

"He ate his mom to *age*," said a voice.

They turned to find Fiona standing at the threshold of the slider doors leading outside. She leaned against the jamb.

"He's shooting for twenty-five or so. He thinks that'll be a perfect age."

"The perfect age for what?" asked Catriona.

Fiona took a wobbly step into the sun. She was pale and shiny as if covered in sweat.

"World domination or whatever."

Catriona took a step toward her. "Are you okay?"

Fiona swallowed. "I don't think so."

Her eyes rolled back in her head, and she fell as Catriona lunged forward to catch her.

CHAPTER EIGHTEEN

"She's shaking," said Anne, snatching a blanket from the back of a chair. She wrapped it around Fiona and helped Catriona move her to the sofa.

Catriona placed a hand on her unresponsive sister's glistening forehead. "She's burning up."

"Does she have the flu?" suggested Jeffrey. He grimaced. "I don't want to get sick."

Anne shot him a scowl. "Get a cold cloth and a glass of water and chicken soup or something. You know the stuff."

Jeffrey, still dripping from being thrown into the pool, slopped out of the room, leaving a trail of water in his wake.

"I haven't been sick in three hundred years," mumbled Anne. "But he'll know what to get."

The comment made Catriona's brow knit. "I never get sick either. Do you?" she asked Broch.

He shook his head. "Nae."

A crackling sound filled the air as Michael materialized wearing his trademark suit. He looked as if he'd flown in from a modeling gig in Milan.

"What's going on here?" he asked, eyeing Fiona. "What happened?"

"Our bloodhound is sick." Anne turned to Con. "What did you do to her?"

Con's eyes widened. "Me? *Nothing.* I mean, I siphoned her a little, but that seemed to be doing her good—"

"How much? How often?" asked Michael.

Con scratched his chin. "Once yesterday, and then today

before we left her place, and then when we got here, she was rarin' to go again—"

Anne's lip curled. "What kind of animals are you?"

Con threw out his hands in mea culpa. "What? I thought I was *fixing* her. You said to talk her into helping us. You said—"

"Typical man," muttered Catriona.

"Seriously," agreed Anne, her glare shifting to Michael.

Speaking of men...

Michael noticed her glaring at him.

"Maybe I should go..." he mumbled.

Anne shook her head. "Whoa there, buddy. Don't even *think* about it. What happened with Rune? He's *free*. Reborn. When were you going to tell us that?"

Con gasped. "Fiona was talking to *Rune*. Maybe he poisoned her." He looked at the Angel. "This is all *Michael's* fault."

All eyes turned to Michael, and his chin lifted in defiance.

"What makes you think Rune is free?" he asked.

"I was just sittin' in a room with him," said Con. "He's a boy, but it's him. Got that nose like a hawk and those blue eyes. He came to recruit Fiona."

Michael held fast for another second before his shoulders slumped a quarter of an inch.

"He...might have escaped."

"I *knew* you were acting suspiciously," growled Anne. "How did it happen?"

Michael sighed. "He held his breath in his cell until he died. No one told us he could do that."

"Held his breath until he died?" echoed Catriona. "That sounds *horrific*. How is that even possible?"

The Angel shook his head. "It's not supposed to be. It took him a few tries."

Catriona winced.

Anne tilted her head back to stare at the ceiling. "This should be getting easier. Instead, we're taking one step forward and a hundred steps back."

"Broch and I will find Rune," said Catriona. "He has a habit of finding *us*. If you can keep an eye on Fiona for me?"

Her tone caught Anne's attention. She sounded confident.

"Can you sense him like your sister?" she asked.

Catriona frowned. "No. Maybe. I'm not sure. But I can check in with Huck Carter—maybe he knows where his *son* is hiding out. If Rune has made himself known, Huck might be terrified of him. He might be *thrilled* to help us save his miserable ass."

Anne looked at Fiona. If Con's poisoning theory was correct, whatever was wrong with Fiona might require Rune to fix it.

Better Catriona and Broch be out looking for Rune than sitting around watching her sister die.

"Go," she said. "Keep us updated."

Catriona and Broch headed out, and Anne turned her focus to Con. "Any thoughts on how you can be useful now that you've killed our tracker?"

"I didn't *kill* her," grumbled Con. He shoved his hands in his pockets and then perked. "Oh, I forgot." He walked to the foyer to where Fiona's purse sat to rifle through it.

"He's going to take this opportunity to rob her?" muttered Michael.

"You don't get to talk," hissed Anne.

Con returned to them with a thumb drive pinched between his fingers.

"This is the list," he announced. "That Joseph character was collecting a master list of sick Kairos in the hopes of building an army. Fiona heard about it while they were holding her and stole it. Her Da's after it, so it must be important."

Anne took the drive from him and tapped it against her chin, mulling the possibilities. "This could come in handy. If and when she gets better, we'll put her on the road. She can confirm the people on the list, and then Catriona and I can sweep in and reboot them."

"You seem to have this under control. I'm going to head back," said Michael. "A lot's going on at headquarters. It's the end of the quarter and—"

"*Whatever*," said Anne. "Try not to free any prisoners on your way out."

He offered a tight smile and then disappeared.

"What an eejit," muttered Con.

Anne frowned at him.

"Shut up and fix your girlfriend."

CHAPTER NINETEEN

When they returned to the Parasol Pictures lot, Catriona climbed into a studio golf cart parked near their apartment instead of heading inside.

"Where are ye goan?" asked Broch. "Wait fer me tae get changed, and ah'll come wit ye."

She shook her head. "I doubt Huck's on the lot. With his wife and kid missing, the cops probably have him waiting on a ransom call or something, but I'm going to go check his soundstage. I'll be right back."

"Ah dinnae lik' ye goan aloon!" he called after her as she sped off. She raised a hand in acknowledgment but didn't slow. She knew how long his showers could last and knew he'd insist on taking one because he never missed a chance.

In the meantime, it seemed like a good idea to knock Huck off her list. Once she confirmed he wasn't on the lot, they could head to his house and see if they could pick up Rune's trail there.

She wheeled to Soundstage Four and moved from the dry heat of the Los Angeles summer into the chill of the cavernous building housing *The Other Side* set. She spotted a familiar set designer fussing with a vignette of casual interview furniture and headed for him.

"Hey, Fletch, is Huck around?"

Fletch finished sliding a table into place in front of a large leather sofa and looked up. "Did you hear about his wife and kid?"

She nodded. "Terrible."

"I know, right? Weird thing is he *is* here. I think he's trying to bury himself in work." He glanced over his shoulder to be sure no one was listening and then leaned in. "Rumor is she left him..."

Catriona wasn't listening to the gossip. She never *dreamed* Huck would be there. Maybe his presence was a sign he *was* under Rune's spell and unconcerned his wife had been reduced to a pile of dust. Or, as Fletch suggested, maybe he was using work to distract himself from the pain.

"Do you know where he is?" she asked.

Fletch pointed behind him. "His office is back there. His name's on the door. *Lucifer.*"

She chuckled, thanked him, and headed to Huck's office to knock on the door.

"Come in," called a voice from inside.

She let herself in. Huck sat on an upholstered chair, flipping through a notebook.

He looked up as she entered.

"Can I help—hey, I know you. What's your name again? Tina?"

"Catriona. Studio security."

He lowered the book in his hands. "Right. If I'd known they had such adorable security here, I would have jumped ship and come to Parasol sooner."

He stared at her as if he expected her to thank him for the compliment. Catriona tried to smile back, hoping to stay on his good side until she extracted the information she needed out of him, but she couldn't stop her lip from curling.

"Sorry to hear about your wife and son," she said.

He frowned. "Terrible thing."

"The police don't want you waiting for a ransom call?" She couldn't stop herself from asking the question. No one in their right mind would go to work after finding their wife and son missing. He had to know *something*.

A thought occurred to her.

Maybe he killed them.

She'd gladly commit all her free time to find evidence against him if the police thought that was the case.

Huck leaned forward as if preparing to share a secret.

"Between you and me, I think she left me. She had some...*issues*."

Catriona nodded.

Like being married to a dirtball.

"Well, if there's anything we can do," she said instead.

Huck pouted like a man who'd been abandoned, but his eyes swept over her body as if he were imagining his new life as a single man.

Catriona tried not to shiver with revulsion.

He folded up his notebook. "I'm, uh, heading back to the house in a second. Came to get my notes. The cops wanted me to go through my recent guest list to see if there was anyone suspicious, just in case."

"Just hand over the whole list," muttered Catriona.

Out loud.

Whoops.

She'd meant to play nice.

It's just so hard.

Huck chuckled and stood. "Was there something you needed?"

Time to be direct.

"I want your son. *Rune.*"

Huck's cheek twitched at the sound of the name.

"Oliver," he corrected.

"I know he's *Rune.* I know who he is and what he is. I just need you to tell me *where* he is."

Huck eyed her. For a moment, he looked as if he'd confess. Then that *hurt* look reappeared on his mug. She wanted to smack his bottom lip right off his face.

"I don't know what you're talking about. But, how do you know my son's nickname?" he asked.

"It was on the drawings on your refrigerator."

Huck couldn't hide his surprise.

"*Sean,*" he said after a moment. "Someone told me the other security guy, Sean, was at my house. Are you working together? Did *you* take my family?"

Catriona rolled her eyes. "*Stop.* You know there was no kidnapping. Are you hiding Rune? Why? He's dangerous. You can't trust him. You'll be next."

"I don't know who you think you are, but I'm reporting you!" Huck's face flushed red, but he'd delivered the line as if he were starring in a bad play. He pretended to look for his phone.

"What if I told you I knew your son killed your wife? Drained her to a pile of ash so he could age up? Would that surprise you? Or did you already know that?"

Huck hemmed a little too long.

Catriona scowled.

He knows.

"You're *nuts*," he said as the book in his lap slid to the ground. He bent to retrieve it. "I'm going to call the cops—"

As he bent, Huck reached around the side of the chair.

Catriona saw it too late.

He's hand reappeared with a baseball bat in it. He swung, clipping her just above her knee. She collapsed, reaching for something to catch herself on but finding nothing.

She'd never dreamed the sniveling little—

Before she could rise, he swung again, his face twisted with fury. She raised her arm to protect her head. The bat glanced off her forearm and clipped the back of her skull.

A burst of fireworks exploded behind Catriona's eyes.

Then everything went black.

CHAPTER TWENTY

Broch was washing his hair with Catriona's vegan keratin-rich coconut and lime-scented shampoo when a feeling came over him. Dread seeped into his bones—a sensation so heavy he stopped working the lather and lowered his hands.

Something's wrong.

A pain shot through his skull, sharp enough that he grunted, and then it was gone with no lingering effect. He felt his head. It was almost as if someone had hit him, but being alone in the shower, that was impossible.

He rinsed without bothering with the conditioner and turned off the water to listen.

Did ah hear somethin'?

Exiting the shower, he called for Catriona.

Nothing.

He grabbed a towel and dried as he padded into the living room, leaving behind a glistening trail of water.

"Catriona?"

She hadn't returned yet.

She said Huck probably wasn't at work.

Why is it takin' sae long?

He glanced at the clock on the microwave. It had been over twenty minutes since she drove off in the golf cart.

Maybe she was talking to someone? Maybe she had other work—

No.

Something was wrong.

He could feel it.

He reentered the bedroom and noticed his kilt hanging on the knob of the closet door.

Perfect.

He wrapped it around him, abandoned a search for a shirt, skipped the elevator, and jogged down the stairs to exit into the payroll office below.

"Oh *my*—"

Jeanie gasped as he jogged past her and out the front door.

"*Thank you for that!*" he heard her call after him.

Broch looked around the corner of the building, searching for signs of the golf cart.

She hadn't returned.

He turned in the direction she'd headed.

Dae ah ken where Huck is?

He didn't.

Never mind.

He'd figure it out.

He jogged until a feeling pulled him to the right as clearly as if someone had jerked a rope tied to his wrist. He turned, speeding his pace.

There it is.

He spotted Catriona's golf cart parked outside Soundstage Four and bolted for the door. Throwing it open, he found the place empty but for a lone man arranging furniture.

Broch trotted down the steps to him.

"Hae ye seen Catriona?" he asked.

The man stopped what he was doing and looked him up and down.

"Who are *you*?" he asked.

"Ah'm her husband," said Broch.

Close enough tae the truth.

The man gaped. "Her husband?" He looked over his shoulder. "You *go*, girl."

"Hae ye seen her?" pressed Broch.

"Oh, yep." He jerked a thumb in the same direction he'd glanced. "She was looking for Huck. His office is back there— name's on the door."

"Thank ye." Broch ran past the man, through a set of doors, and down a long hallway. Halfway down it, he spotted the door with Huck's name on it and pounded on it with his fist.

"Catriona?"

No answer came, so he tried the knob. It was locked.

He grimaced, knowing Catriona would be *furious* with him

for destroying the door, but his feeling of dread had been growing into something more akin to *fear,* and it would not be denied.

Broch slammed his shoulder into the door. It popped open and bounced off the wall behind it. He stopped it from hitting him with his palm.

The room was empty.

Huck's dressing room was small and unoccupied. There was no place to hide. He was about to leave when he stopped mid-spin, his gaze dropping to a crimson smear breaking the pattern of the rug laying in front of the sofa. He squatted and touched his fingers to it.

Blood.

He smelled something—*pine?*—but obnoxiously strong—something like the fluid Catriona used to clean things.

Someone had tried to wash the floor and missed the spot on the rug.

His fear turned to panic.

Broch returned to the hallway. The man out front hadn't seen Huck or Catriona leave, so he jogged in the opposite direction to a door with a glowing exit sign above it. He pushed through it into a parking lot.

Broch raised his hand to shield his eyes as he scanned the lot.

There.

He spotted an SUV backing out of a spot, ten parking spots down on his right. Near it sat a rolling laundry bin. He'd seen ones like it before—the studio used them to collect wash.

They'd make an excellent way tae shift a body.

The SUV finished backing and started toward him.

Broch stepped out in front of it and held up his hand.

"*Stop!*" he roared.

The SUV slowed for a moment and then jumped forward, continuing toward him.

Yer nae goin' anywhere.

When the vehicle was nearly upon him, Broch threw himself on the hood, his fingers sinking into the gutter the windshield wipers called home.

Through the glass, he saw Huck Carter staring back at him, eyes wide.

"*Ah said stop!*" he commanded.

The engine revved as Huck hit the gas.

Broch gripped the SUV with his left hand and raised his right in the air. He pounded the windshield with the side of his fist, and the glass splintered into a thousand tiny cracks but didn't give.

Before he could strike a second time, Huck swerved hard to the left. Broch used both hands to keep his perch. The bare skin of his torso helped him stick to the hood better than cloth would have allowed, but as Huck snaked down the parking aisle, it was all he could do to keep from being thrown.

Huck straightened the vehicle. Broch found his grip and raised his fist to finish off the windshield.

His hand still hovered in the air when Huck slammed on the brakes.

Och.

He hadn't seen that coming.

No grip could hold him in place—certainly not the fingers of one hand. Broch flipped up, his back slamming into the glass and knees bending over the roof.

Huck hit the gas again. The glass Broch felt buckling beneath him held and Broch slid up and over the roof until he felt roof nomore.

Only *air.*

The feeling of flying didn't last.

He hit the ground behind the vehicle, shoulder first, *hard.*

The wind had been knocked out of him as he landed, and his skull bounced on the asphalt.

Broch pushed aside the pain and scrambled to his feet.

Twenty feet ahead of him, the SUV's tires squealed as it rounded a corner and disappeared.

He broke into a sprint.

CHAPTER TWENTY-ONE

Huck drove miles into the hills and then pulled over. He couldn't keep driving. His windshield was shattered—not only could he barely see through it, but if a cop spotted him, he'd be pulled over for sure.

Little chance they wouldn't find Catriona in the back. He didn't know if the bitch was awake or dead or *what*.

He stepped out of the vehicle to get some air and call Oliver, er, *Rune*. It didn't matter if Rune was some ancient time traveler who'd aged five years in a day. It was still hard not to think of him as Oliver sometimes.

Rune answered.

"Thank God. I need your help," said Huck.

"What is wrong with you?"

Huck scowled. "Oliver?"

"*Rune.*"

"Yeah, whatever. Your voice is so low—?"

Rune sniffed. "My body is approximately twenty years old now."

"Really?" Huck tried to imagine his son as a man. A tiny part of him ached to see his little boy again. Very tiny. Sometimes, he couldn't deny it felt odd knowing he'd never see that weird little kid again.

He shook away the feeling. It made sense for Rune to accelerate his aging. It would be hard for a six-year-old boy to command the respect of an army—if that really was his plan—and he'd be more useful *now* when Huck desperately needed his help.

He could drive now? Maybe pick him up—

"What do you want?" snapped Rune.

"Huh? Oh. Catriona, the, uh, security gal from the lot. She *knows*. She was looking for you, and I hit her. She's in my trunk. What should I do with her?"

"Who?"

"*Catriona*. Security at Parasol. I think I heard she's Fiona Duffy's sister...? Someone told me that... Isn't that *your* Fiona?" Huck trailed off as he did the math. "Wait, that would make *her* your daughter, too?"

"Fiona? You found Fiona?"

"No. *Catriona*. I hit her—" Huck huffed. "This crazy big guy in a skirt came out of nowhere and jumped on my car and broke my windshield—"

"What do you want? I'm busy."

Huck growled. "This is your fault. This happened to me while trying to protect *you*. What should I do with the woman in my trunk?"

"I don't care. Bury her."

"She's not—" Huck glanced at the car. "I don't think...? *No*. I need you to come here and do that dust thing to her. That'll take care of the evidence."

"I already have someone in my sights. I told you. I'm *busy*."

"Rune—"

Huck heard the phone disconnect.

"Rune!"

He called back. It went to voicemail.

"*Dammit!*"

Huck raised his phone with plans to dash it to the street and then thought better of it. He leaned his back against the SUV. His chin pressed against his chest.

"Okay, think, think, *think*..."

Something made him glance to his left.

Oh no.

His eyes bugged.

It can't be.

Running over the hill at what seemed like an impossible speed was a man.

A *giant*.

Huck recognized him.

"Who *is* this guy?" he spat aloud.

He scrambled to get back into his Escalade, but before he could put it into gear, his side window shattered, and an enormous hand grabbed his shirt.

Oh shit—

Huck wrenched sideways, trying to break free as broken glass raked the side of his throat.

The driver-side door opened, and he spilled onto the asphalt.

Gasping for breath, Huck squinted up at the backlit form of the half-naked monster standing over him.

"Who are you?" he croaked.

He tried to stand as the man moved to the back of his SUV. He felt weak. His hand rose to his throat.

Wet.

That's not good.

He flopped back to the ground and looked at his fingers.

They were bright with blood.

Not good at all.

CHAPTER TWENTY-TWO

Catriona crouched in the back of the SUV, her head ringing. She'd awoken when the vehicle stopped. Something was going on outside. She had to be ready. This could be her one chance to get away.

She prayed she didn't jump out and fall flat on her face. She still felt woozy. It was hard to stay awake.

The back hatch opened.

Steadying herself against the side of the vehicle, she kicked out, aiming for *crotch*.

She connected.

The man groaned. He backed away and doubled over as she scrambled out of the car and *ran*.

Her head was swimming. She forced her legs to move and tried not to run into anything that would slow her progress. Though she found it hard to focus, she did her best to divine her location.

The ground sloped.

The Hills— ?

"Catriona!"

Catriona slowed.

I know that voice.

She glanced back.

Broch stood at the back of the vehicle she'd been in, standing bent over and looking as if he were trying to catch his breath.

As if he'd been kicked in the crotch.

The act of glancing back turned out to be too much for her already terrible balance. She stumbled sideways like a drunk and caught herself against a bushy tree before sliding to the ground.

"Are ye okay?" called Broch.

Catriona propped her back against the elderberry, catching her breath with her eyes closed.

"Yes." She stood and walked back to the SUV, her head aching. As she grew closer, she noticed a body lying on the ground beside the driver-side door.

"Is that Huck?" she asked, adjusting her trajectory to head toward him.

Broch straightened. "Aye."

They met at the side of the Escalade to stare at where Huck had crumpled. Blood pooled next to his head and ran through the fingers of the hand he had pressed against his throat.

"What happened to him?" asked Catriona.

"The glass?" suggested Broch. His eyes were wide like the innocent babe she knew he wasn't.

"Did you jerk his head through the window?"

He shrugged.

"Do you have your phone? We need to call an ambulance—"

Huck reached out and clamped his hand around Catriona's ankle. Startled, she looked down and saw a ghastly smile, his teeth red with blood.

Then he disappeared.

Completely.

Catriona gasped.

I must be worse off than I thought.

She looked at Broch.

"Did he just disappear?"

Broch nodded. "Aye."

She let out a sigh as her sludgy brain realized what Huck's disappearance *meant*.

"He's one of *us*," she said. She put her hand against her head. She wanted to remove her skull and put it aside for a while.

"Ah didnae ken," said Broch.

"I know you didn't know. Which, I might add, makes the fact you *killed* him even worse." She frowned at him as best she could without wobbling. "What did I tell you about killing people?"

He shrugged again. "He'd taken ye."

"It's not that I'm not grateful." She leaned against him, and he put his arm around her to pull her closer.

"Are ye okay?" he asked. "Yer heid…"

"Hurts." She knew she looked like a horror show. She could feel the blood crusting in her hair, pulling at the follicles.

"I'd better call Sean." Her gaze ran from the blood on the asphalt to Huck's truck and back again.

"We need a clean-up on aisle four."

CHAPTER TWENTY-THREE

Fiona gasped and sat up.

Where am I?

It took her a moment to focus, but the room was familiar to her.

Anne's house.

She was on the sofa. The skin on her face felt strange and crusty. She heard a snort and looked to her left to find Con sitting in a chair beside her, snoring.

"*Con.*" She said, reaching out to touch his knee.

He jumped and snorted again as he awoke.

"What? Where?"

"You were asleep."

He blinked at her. "You're awake, lass."

She nodded. "How did I end up falling asleep on the sofa? And why do I feel so gross and clammy?"

He sat up. "You had a fever and passed out. It was touch and go there for a bit—we almost took you to the hospital. How do you feel?"

She swung her legs around and sat up. "Fine, I guess. I feel—" What was it? There was something different. She felt...*happy?*

She looked at him.

"I don't know. I feel *good.*"

"Good. Good." He reached out and touched her face. "Yer fever broke."

Fiona reached up and tried to fluff her hair. "I must look crazy. I'm going to freshen up."

Feeling wobbly, she walked to the foyer to retrieve her purse and then continued to the downstairs powder room. She stared at herself in the mirror.

Yikes.

She powdered her nose and applied lipstick to lose the *corpse bride* look she was rockin'.

When she returned the makeup to her purse, she noticed the thumb drive was still there.

The list.

She plucked it out and returned to the living room to hold it out for Con.

"The list?" he asked, eyeing it.

She nodded.

"I was keeping it to use it for myself, but..." She searched her mind for answers but found only a blank stretch of grassy plain where her devious plans once grew.

"Wildflowers," she said.

Con's eyebrows bobbed upward. "What's that now?"

"I feel cured," she said. "It's like I had all this anger writhing around inside my head—like a ball of black snakes— and now I see *wildflowers.*"

Con's brow knit. "You didn't get into the cold medicine before you woke me up, did you?"

She chuckled. "*No.*"

"Well then, that's fine then, innit?"

Still feeling weak, she lowered herself into a chair. "I think Rune did something to me. When I was little. I think he planted this infection in me—"

"And you just sweat it out?"

She perked. "I think I *did.*" She held out the drive. "Take it. Seriously."

He cupped her hand in his but didn't take the drive.

"Deary, I think it's wonderful ye want to give it to us, but we copied it the second ye passed out. Anne's upstairs with the Angel right now, formulatin' a plan for tracking them all down."

Fiona smiled sheepishly and dropped the thumb drive on top of a pile of magazines laying on the table. "Of *course,* you did."

"But there *is* something we need ye to do if ye would?" he added.

She sniffed. "What's that?"

"If you think you can still sense him, we need you to find Rune before he does what he did to *you* to the whole world."

She nodded.

"That would be my *pleasure*."

CHAPTER TWENTY-FOUR

Snuffling?

The word floated through his mind before he knew why.

Huck Carter opened his eyes.

Something wet tickled his left ear in the unsettling way a spider might run up an arm during the middle of the night. He rolled to his side, slapping at the side of his head.

A dog jumped away from him, startled by his movement. Evidently satisfied Huck wasn't trying to hurt him, he sat and stared.

Huck stared back at him.

Why am I on the ground with a dog?

He looked around. He was in a walled backyard. The tan dog was loose, but it wasn't large nor scary. Some kind of Labrador mixed with something smaller. A swing set with three seats, one broken and dangling, sat in the corner. The home was a rancher, with a wonky back screen door and a collection of toys piled against the foundation.

Where am I?

He looked down at his body. He was covered with dust, wearing the clothes he'd put on that morning. He felt his pockets and located his phone. Pulling it out, he checked the date.

Same day still.

He remembered getting dressed that morning, but the rest of the day was fuzzy...

How had he ended up in someone's backyard?

His throat ached, and he raised his hand to touch it. *Wet.* He looked at his fingers. Not red, not blood—oh, *the dog*. The dog had been licking his throat, where the skin felt rough and raw.

The flash of a man chasing him blinked against the wall of Huck's mind. Long hair. *Big.* Shirtless. Chugging at him like a locomotive.

Wearing a skirt?

No, a kilt.

The details of his day came rushing back to him. The woman who worked at the studio, *Catriona.* Once he pictured her face, the rest began to fall into place.

She'd been poking around. She knew too much. Somehow, she knew about Rune. He'd struck her with a baseball bat signed by half the eighty-seven Red Sox.

I hope I didn't ruin that bat...

He'd tried to get her off the Parasol lot, then that monster man jumped on his Escalade—probably dented the hood. He'd gotten away, pulled over, tried to reach Rune—and then the big guy came running over the hill like some kind of Terminator cyborg, smashed his window, and pulled his head through it.

The glass slid across his throat—

Oh.

Now, he remembered.

He'd been laying on the ground bleeding—

But, *wait*—there was a silver lining.

It worked.

Usually, if he were dying, he'd transport to wherever time took him. But, this time, he'd been concentrating *very* hard on returning to *this* time, like Rune had explained to him.

Turns out he'd been listening to the freak.

And it *worked.*

Sonuvabitch.

He'd also tried to concentrate on *Rune* himself, so he'd be transported to him, but unless Rune had come back a second time as a lab mix—

"What are you doing over there?" said a voice.

Huck turned to see Rune's face peering over the wall at him. At least, he assumed it was Rune. His son had been six a day ago, around thirteen the last time he saw him, and now he looked to be in his early twenties.

But those eyes.

There was no mistaking those eyes.

"You're *here*," said Huck.

"And you're *there*. I felt you show up. It took me twenty

minutes to find you. Get over here."

Huck stood. The dog padded over to him, and he patted it on the head before exiting the backyard through a gate and walking to the front of the house next door.

He looked up and down the street. It wasn't a great neighborhood.

Rune opened the door and let him inside.

The house fit the neighborhood. He could tell it hadn't been updated since the nineties, and half the furniture harkened from a time long before *that*. Everything felt very *brown*.

"Why here?" he asked as he entered.

"Why did you jump?" asked Rune.

Rune didn't seem as disturbed about the house's disgusting state.

I knew he wasn't my kid.

"Why didn't you tell me you were one of *us* when you were a kid?" asked Huck. "It would have explained...a *lot*."

"I only realized who I was recently. Remember that day I wandered out of recess and walked all the way home?"

Huck chuckled at the memory. His wife had called him "frantic."

"You scared Ashley to *death*."

Rune studied him with his blank stare, so he continued. "Yeah. Anyhow, I get it. I've been reborn twice. Did you know *I* was one of *you*?"

"No one is *me*," said Rune.

"Right. I mean in *general*."

Rune sniffed. "If you must know, I concentrated on finding rebirth with someone who would be useful to me. It turned out to be you." Rune's mouth twisted into something that resembled a smile. "Between your network of followers and my sheer power—"

Huck frowned. He thought he'd been doing pretty well with his own power grab, but this Rune guy was some kind of Lex Luthor with a *world domination* master plan.

He had no intention of playing second fiddle to some blue-eyed freak, but *now* wasn't the time to make his move. He'd play along until he had a better idea where things were headed. He needed to know more about Rune's powers and plans. Maybe he'd steal them. Maybe he'd help and then get rid of the guy.

"Why did you have to jump?" Rune asked again.

"Jump? Oh, you mean how'd I die?" Huck paused to gather his thoughts. "A woman came to my dressing room talking about you—she knew too much. I panicked and hit her with a bat."

"You hit her with a flying rat?"

"A *baseball* bat."

Rune grunted. "Ah. Continue."

"Do you know her? Her name's Catriona. She works at the studio."

Rune seemed to drift off, so Huck plowed ahead. "Anyway, I took her off the lot and—wait—I *called* you. I asked you for help, remember? You hung up on me."

"I was busy."

"Yeah. Well, thanks for that, because two seconds later, this giant Highlander-looking—"

Rune straightened. "Highlander?"

"Yes. Damndest thing. He was wearing a kilt and nothing else. He came barreling over the hill—"

"You saw the Highlander? Why didn't you call me?"

Huck gritted his teeth. "I *did* call you. *You hung up.*"

"The Highlander is our sworn enemy."

Huck turned his palms to the ceiling. "This is all news to me, *Rune.* You need to keep me in the loop if you want me doing things a certain way."

"Where is he now?"

"I don't know. After he was done *killing me* I'm assuming he took the woman out of the back of my—" He stopped, his eyes growing wide. "My *SUV.* She's probably sending the cops to my Escalade right now. Or *he* is. Oh, *God.* What if she's dead? They're going to be looking for me. I shouldn't have come back *here*—"

He stopped as his gaze settled on a pile of ash heaped on a lounge chair positioned in front of a television. The television was so old and so thick that it looked more like a wood-paneled refrigerator.

Huck recognized the tiny pyramid from the similar pile he'd found at home. The pile that used to be his wife.

Poor Ashley. When she won runner-up in the Miss Georgia pageant, she certainly never imagined she'd end up a pile of ash heaped on a twenty-thousand-dollar rug somewhere in Los Angeles. Funny, because that's close to how her parents said she'd end up if she moved to this *devil town* with him.

"Did you do that?" he asked, motioning to the pile. "Anyone I know, or are you branching out from my immediate family?"

Rune's expression soured. "She was old. I only gained about six months from her. But I was tired and wanted a place to rest."

Huck studied the heap. "Can I do that? Turn people to ash, Old Testament-style?"

Rune cocked his head. "How old are you?"

"Number of years on the planet at any age and any time?" Huck considered the question. "I don't know. It's a lot of math, and there are gaps. I've got some fuzzy memories of being in Victorian England. I think I was a Duke."

Rune studied his fingernails. "Four hundred thirty-six B.C."

"What's that?"

"My earliest memory."

"Really? You started that early or jumped back that early."

He sniffed. "*Started*, my boy."

"Hm. So you've developed *special* powers? Like some old vampire king or something?"

Rune didn't bother to answer, opting instead to shift topics. "I need to be on your show tonight."

"What? Did you not hear me? The cops are probably looking for me. My television days are *over*."

"They're not."

"How do you figure?"

Rune reached out and slapped him on the neck, directly on the rugged, tender spot below his left ear where he'd torn his throat open on the window.

"*Ow*." Huck stepped back, holding his throat. "What is wrong with you?"

"I assume that bled when it happened?"

"*Yes*. Enough that I *died*—"

"You think the Highlander will lead the authorities to a pool of *your* blood?" Rune sniffed. "I don't think so."

Huck sucked in air to retort and then paused.

The freak had a good point. Maybe he wasn't quite as dumb as he seemed.

"So you think they'll keep everything to themselves?"

"Absolutely. He has as many secrets to guard as you do."

"*They*. There's Catriona, too."

Huck ignored him and sighed.

He felt a little better.

"I need you to arrange my interview for tonight," said Rune.

Huck shook his head. "Hold on. Even if you're right about the blood, I can't put you on tonight."

"Why not?"

"Why not? First of all, I'd have to bump someone last minute. Second, *why?* Why do you want to be on the show?"

"I need to call my minions to me. One in particular."

"Your—" Huck decided not to waste time questioning the *minion* bit. "Who?"

"I remember a name from Jonathan's list. He singled him out as a warrior. One to rival the Highlander. I need him *here.* I need him by my side for protection."

"And you want to get a message to him using my show?"

"Yes. I need to send a message to him and to tell the others to prepare for battle."

Huck walked around the chair covered in ash and planted his tush on the arm of the sofa. He hated touching anything in the house, but he was exhausted.

"What battle?" he asked as he rubbed his temples.

"Survival of the fittest. We're going to start culling the weak. *Faster.*"

Huck looked up.

That's it.

Rune had put what he'd felt in his bones for so long into words.

"Survival of the fittest," he echoed. "That's what I've been preaching in so many words."

"It's in your *blood,*" said Rune.

"So you want me to bring you on as the leader of a new group striving to make America stronger?"

"The *world* stronger," corrected Rune.

Huck held up a hand. "Right. But let's start with America."

He smiled.

"Trust me."

CHAPTER TWENTY-FIVE

Catriona sat staring at the enormous television mounted to the wall of Anne's cavernous living room. The volume was off. She wasn't paying attention to *anything* except feeling better after taking a baseball bat to the skull.

Mortifying.

She wasn't sure what felt worse; her head or the knowledge that that smug little rat Huck Carter had got the drop on her.

How was she supposed to know he kept a bat behind his sofa?

A bat? Why?

Safe at Anne's, she'd sat in a comfy chair, *staying awake* with Broch staring at her, his face twisted with concern, for *two hours.* After two hours, she demanded he find something else to do. She couldn't take him pacing around the room like an expectant father.

She stretched and cracked her neck. Her head *did* feel better. She couldn't think of a time she'd been happier to heal faster than most people.

Concussions *sucked.*

Who knew?

It was time to cover their tracks and mop up the fallout.

She and Broch had taken Huck's Escalade to a lonely section of town and left it there with the keys inside. She'd used an energy drink she'd found rolling around under the seat to wash away some of the blood. It wasn't perfect, but it made it a little less obvious that someone had been jerked through the window against their will—and their *throat slit.*

Tomorrow, they'd deal with Huck's disappearance. His

wife and son had gone missing, and then *he* went missing, too? The police would have some questions. No matter what story they spun, there would be scandal and investigations. Huck was rich and famous and starred on live television every weeknight—there was no way to pretend he'd left town for better pastures.

Eh. They'd think of something. She wasn't too worried about it. She and Sean would find a way to keep the blowback away from themselves and Parasol because that's what they *did*. They'd been in worse predicaments.

Maybe.

At least, there was *no* chance of anyone finding any bodies. Ashley had lived up to her name, Huck was in some other time, and Rune was getting older by the second.

They had another thing working in their favor—Huck's guests were all such vile people that the cops wouldn't run out of potential suspects until the end of the century.

Sean was already on it. He'd been alongside Broch, fawning over her rattled head, until he got the call from the studio about how Huck hadn't shown up for rehearsal. He was out "looking" for the weasel now.

Hopefully, Huck had spun far into the past where no modern comforts existed. Hopefully, some suspicious townsfolk had seen him appear out of nowhere. Perhaps, he was currently on trial for being a witch—*no, scratch that.* She didn't want him dying—that might send him right back into their laps.

Maybe he could just sit in a nice dark prison for a few decades...

Catriona's attention shifted as Fiona entered with a stemmed glass of red wine dangling from her fingers.

"Hey, how's the head?" she asked, sitting on the sofa.

"Better. How are you?"

Fiona smiled. "Never better."

Fiona said the words as if they'd surprised her. It felt to Catriona her entire aura had changed. It was never wise to give her sister the benefit of the doubt. Still, she was starting to believe Fiona *was* a kinder, gentler version of her former self.

Apparently, Con really *did* have a magic willy.

"Tomorrow, I was thinking, we'd start hunting Dad," suggested Fiona.

Catriona nodded. "Sounds like a plan."

She did her best not to look worried. She knew they'd have to get rid of Rune before he caused more trouble, but her to-do list was beginning to feel endless.

Fiona's gaze wandered to middle-distance as she sipped her wine. She looked pensive.

"Are you sure you're okay with rebooting Rune?" asked Catriona. She refused to call him *Dad*.

Fiona straightened. "Nothing would make me happier." She attempted to smile, but the wistful look crept back into her expression.

"Can I be honest?" she asked.

Catriona chuckled. "It would be refreshing."

Fiona let the comment pass and raised her glass to her lips. "I'm *embarrassed*."

"About being an evil bitch for the last few years?"

Fiona snorted wine through her nose and sputtered. "Damn..." She wiped her face on the back of her hand and took a minute to find her composure. "*Yes*. I've been so single-minded—" She chopped the air in front of her as if carving a path through it. "And now, everything that was *so* important to me seems *crazy*."

Catriona laughed. "I could have told you you were crazy any time. I think I *did*, actually..."

Fiona huffed. "Watch it. You better appreciate what you've got. I'm not going to apologize *forever*. I'm feeling particularly warm and fuzzy today, but I'm still *me*."

"Okay. I won't push my luck." She glanced at the television to see Huck Carter's opening credits. They'd decided to plow ahead with the show in his absence.

"I guess they got a guest host," she mumbled to herself. She hadn't heard anything from Sean, and she'd been curious to see how Parasol would handle Huck's disappearance. No one knew he was gone for good yet, of course. She and Sean couldn't hint to the producers that it might be time to start looking for another job or find themselves another host without looking either guilty or psychic.

The studio would no doubt task her, Sean, and Luther with finding Huck. Since finding him was impossible, they could instead put the time toward other things, like traveling the country with Fiona the Bloodhound rebooting screwed up Kairos.

Perfect.

She could use a road trip.

Being in L.A. too long made people weird.

The screen shifted to a shot of Huck sitting at his news desk with the phrase, "Does America need to get stronger?" superimposed over the bottom of the screen.

Catriona's brow knit.

That's not a guest host.

Rerun?

Huck babbled on in silence because she had the volume off.

Catriona reached for the remote as the camera panned back to reveal Huck's guest sitting to his left.

"Holy shit," said Fiona, fumbling her wine glass.

Catriona gasped and turned up the volume.

"So, Rune, tell us a little more about you. You're the head of a group advocating for the survival of the fittest, is that right?" said Huck in his trademark whiney tone.

"This has to be *live*," said Catriona.

Fiona agreed. "You said Huck was gone."

"He *was*. Broch *wrecked* him. He disappeared in front of my eyes, complete with a flashing light—I assumed he'd be swept somewhere far away in time, but—"

"Not so far away," muttered Fiona, raising her glass to her lips.

Catriona was starting to think she'd need a glass of wine, too. None of this made sense.

No, there was *one* possibility.

"He must have the same skills as Rune. He must be able to pick where he goes."

Fiona nodded. "And he came right back here like a rat-faced boomerang."

"Right. Lucky us."

Fiona's head cocked. "Does he have all of Rune's skills? Can he eat people? Is *he* the one who killed his wife?"

Catriona paused the television and looked at her sister, horrified at the idea they now had *two* powerful enemies.

Fiona looked pouty.

"What's *that* face?" Catriona asked.

"Nothing. It just seems like everyone can drain people except *me*."

Catriona shook her head. "*I* can't. *Broch* can't."

"I mean everyone on Team Evil."

"You're not on Team Evil anymore."

She huffed. "Can't I be a *little* bit evil? Maybe steal a *little* life from someone now and again to smooth out the crow's feet and tighten the old jawline?" Fiona slapped under her chin with the back of her hand.

"What's wrong with aging gracefully?"

Fiona looked at her like she'd grown a second head.

"In *Hollywood*?"

Catriona hit record to ensure they had a copy of Rune's interview and then resumed watching. Rune was terrible on camera—wooden, mumbly—but his intentions were clear enough.

He was gathering his troops.

"He's calling them to action," said Catriona, motioning to the screen. "The people on Joseph's list."

Rune pled for his people to join him before trailing off in some other language Catriona didn't recognize.

Fiona scowled. "Does he have a copy of the list? He said he needed it from me."

Catriona shook her head. "It doesn't sound like it. This is more of a generalized plea."

The camera flipped back to Huck.

"If you're one of Rune's ah, *minions*, you can go to our website to download his instructions now on how to make the most of your, er, *powers*."

Huck was doing his best to play both sides. He *knew* everything Rune said was true, but he still wanted to act dubious enough about the idea of time-travelers that his producers didn't send him for counseling. Maybe he was afraid if he acted *too* enthusiastic about Rune's ramblings, the network would yank him.

Though, why *this* would be the thing that got him canceled after *years* of hideous shows, she couldn't imagine.

"We need to tell Anne," said Catriona.

Fiona stood. "I'm out of wine. I'll find her and send her your way. Have you seen Con?"

Catriona clucked her tongue. "Give it a rest. You're *cured* already."

Fiona giggled and headed out of the room, passing Broch as he entered. He held half a sandwich in his paw.

"She looks lik' she's feeling better," said Broch, motioning behind him as Fiona passed. His attention shifted to the television, and he lowered his sandwich to point at the screen.

"Isnae that—"

"The guy you killed. Yep. And wait until you see who's beside him."

The camera switched to Rune. Broch's eyes bugged.

"Na—"

Rune leaned forward to stare into the camera as if he could see someone on the other side.

"Gog, I need you to come to me. I need you by my side. I have a special mission for you. You will slay the Highlander and—"

"Whoa, okay, we've got it," said Huck as the camera switched to him. "I'm sure you mean a *metaphorical* slaying, right?"

"No," said Rune offscreen. "I mean it quite literally—"

"Okay, well, thank you for stopping by, and Gog, if you're out there, Rune's waiting for you. Next up, wait until you hear who should be going to jail if I have anything to say about it..."

Catriona stood. "If we go to the studio now, we might be able to catch Huck and Rune and take care of them for good."

Broch bit into his sandwich, nodding.

"Who's Gog?"

CHAPTER TWENTY-SIX

County Jail, Somewhere in Ohio

Gog stood to his full height of six-foot-nine inches, his attention locked on the small television mounted to the ceiling, where Rune spoke into the camera.

The blue-eyed, hawk-nosed man stared at him as if he could see into his soul.

Gog couldn't believe it.

He's calling me.

He'd wandered to the rec area to watch television. A handful of other prisoners sat in chairs around the screen. Others milled around or chatted at one of the gathering tables. A guard stood at the doorway with his back to them.

"Hey, Gog, you think he's talking about you?" asked a gap-toothed man sitting on a bench not far from him.

Gog nodded. "It's time. He's here. I've been called."

"I don't know how many other people are named *Gog*," said another man, chuckling. "*Must* be him."

"Freak," muttered someone.

Gog turned.

His gaze settled on a young man he knew as *Chili* sitting behind him.

The boy's face went white.

Chili knew he'd been heard. Or he didn't. Maybe it hadn't even been him. Gog was used to people talking about him.

They were scared.

They didn't understand his power.

At eighteen, he'd had demon fangs tattooed around his

mouth, so it looked as if he had a monster mouth full of razor-sharp teeth. On his head, he inked horns that curled over his ears like a ram's.

On the top of his dome, he had one word printed in thick black gothic lettering:

GOG

If he let his hair and beard grow out, the tattoos disappeared, but in prison, he shaved both to be sure everyone saw. He wanted to be sure everyone knew he was *Gog*.

Gog leaned over his chair, grabbed the young man by the throat, and pulled him to his feet. Chili called out for help as best he could as Gog turned him like a rag doll and tucked him into a chokehold. The other prisoners scrambled to get away, knocking over chairs and each other in their haste.

"Big guy's lost it," said someone.

"*Stop*," begged Chili, gagging. "Let *go*." He slapped and punched and kicked, but he was no match for Gog.

The guard at the door turned to see what the commotion was about. He smacked an alarm and rushed into the room, fumbling to pull his pistol from his holster.

Gog dragged the boy until his back was against the wall.

"You put him down, Gog," commanded the guards as more officers appeared with rifles in hand.

Gog shook the boy to show the hold he had on his throat. "I'm going to kill him. You better shoot me."

"We don't need to do that," said one of the rifle-toting guards. "Let him go, and we'll forget all about this."

"*Shoot*," squawked Chili.

Gog squeezed tighter. "I'm going to break his windpipe."

Chili slapped at his arm.

Gog shifted to be sure Chili's body covered most of his own and tucked his head behind the boy's, leaving his chest as the clearest shot.

"I won't stop until you shoot me," he told them.

Gog heard a *snap*. Something gave way in Chili's throat.

Chili went limp.

"He doesn't have much longer," lied Gog.

The kid was dead.

The guards took steady aims.

"This is your last chance. I'm going to kill you," said the chattiest guard.

Gog grinned, his demon teeth stretching around his

mouth.

That's the point.

Two more guards arrived.

Gog closed his eyes and concentrated.

Los Angeles.

Highlander.

He would go to Rune with the Highlander's head in a bag.

He would give it to him as a gift.

As an *offering.*

Gog made a move to make it clear he was crushing the life out of Chili.

The trick worked.

Guns fired.

CHAPTER TWENTY-SEVEN

Anne, Catriona, and Broch pulled up to Parasol in Anne's Range Rover. Catriona commandeered a golf cart and drove them the rest of the way to Soundstage Four, nervous energy coursing through her body. Her head didn't hurt anymore. The sight of Rune and Huck together on television had knocked self-pity out of her.

Now, she could only think about one thing—sending them both *away*.

She pulled in front of Huck's building to the sound of screeching tires. Before they could spill out of the cart, Huck stepped through the door to greet them as if he'd been waiting for them. Leading his arrival was a large man who seemed to be fifty-percent biceps.

"Hey, kids," said Huck. "Have you met Delmont? He's my personal bodyguard. Got to be safe, you know?"

Catriona scowled. Delmont had a bald head like a bullet and an iron cross blackening his right forearm. She felt confident Broch could take him, but her job was to *stop* drama on the lot, not be the source of it.

Sensing trouble, a small crowd of Parasol staff collected in the area, eyes locked on the standoff between Huck, his pet giant, and Catriona's crew.

Sean wheeled up in a golf cart of his own.

"Get back to work," he commanded the looky-loos. Some left. Some didn't. Some pretended only to assume fallback positions with phones raised to record.

Great.

Anything they did would end up on social media an hour from now.

Sean moved to Catriona's side.

"We can't do this here," he said in a low voice.

Catriona sighed. "I *know*. I was hoping to catch him in the parking lot."

"Did you say parking lot?" asked Huck, barking a laugh. "I won't be making *that* mistake again. FYI, they found my Escalade stripped to the bone. Thanks for that. I'll send you the bill for the new one."

"Be sure to hold your breath for our check," said Catriona. "Seriously. Start now. It can be done. Talk to Rune."

"Where *is* Rune?" asked Anne.

Huck leered at her. "Who do we have here?" He dragged his gaze up and down her body. "Does the carpet match the drapes?"

Anne lowered a whither gaze on the man.

"Wow. That is original." Her fist curled, and she glanced at Sean. "You're *sure* we can't do this here?"

Sean shook his head. "No. Let's go."

"*Bye*," said Huck, waving with only his fingers. He slapped Delmont on the shoulder before re-entering the studio with the big guy on his heels.

"One sword to the head," muttered Anne. "He drops, we grab him, *done*."

"And how would you explain it if he disappeared out from under you?" asked Sean.

Anne shrugged. "Special effects?"

Catriona's head cocked. "She might be on to something—"

"*No*," said Sean. "There will be a better time." He pulled at his salt-and-pepper chin whiskers. "It's late. Let's sleep on it and come up with a plan tomorrow. A real plan. One that takes care of *all* our loose ends."

"Lik' Gog?" asked Broch.

Sean frowned. "I saw that. I was out pretending to look for the idiot, and nobody bothered to tell me he was *here* filming a damn show. I'm afraid to ask what a Gog is."

"It can't be good," agreed Catriona. "I don't think anyone ever named a puppy or a unicorn *Gog*."

Sean nudged a still-smoldering Anne with his elbow. "I'm heading to Luther's for the night. Can I offer you a ride to your car?"

She nodded. "Thanks." She turned to Catriona and Broch. "Swing by the house around eight tomorrow morning? I'll have

Jeffrey make his famous French toast."

"Ah'll be there," said Broch, a little too quickly.

Food was a close second to scented soaps on his favorites list.

Anne hopped into Sean's golf cart as Catriona and Broch headed back to their apartments in hers. Broch took her hand as she drove.

"Say the word, and ah'll smash Huck's teeth tae a fine paste."

"That sounds *awesome*, but no, Sean's right. We can pick a better time."

She squeezed his hand, happy to have him near.

Things *could* be worse.

She could be doing all of this *alone*.

She parked the cart, and they took the elevator to their apartments. Catriona paused at her door.

"Do you want to come in? Maybe have a drink?"

Broch smiled. "Aye."

She wondered how much longer they were going to pretend they lived in different apartments.

She let them inside, bending to retrieve the mail Jeanie had slid under her door. She shuffled through it, pausing on an envelope with a familiar address in Las Vegas.

"This is from the wedding chapel," she said, opening it. She pulled out the single sheet and scanned over it.

"Whit is it?" asked Broch.

She handed it to him.

"We're not married," she said.

"Whit?" he took the sheet and read it.

"I knew there'd been a mistake. We never signed any state licenses or anything. Looks like they got us mixed up with another couple."

Broch looked up at her.

He seemed sad.

"Bit ah lik'd being yer husband," he moaned in a comically whiney voice.

She giggled. "We knew it was a mistake. No biggie." She dropped the rest of the mail on the counter. "I'll be right back. I'm going to get a quick shower."

She walked into her bedroom feeling a little sad as well.

She knew she wasn't married to Broch, but it still felt like a loss to be told *officially*—

"Mebbe ah should join ye?" called Broch.
She grinned.
"Aye, maybe ye should."

CHAPTER TWENTY-EIGHT

Broch put the letter down on the counter and watched Catriona walk into the bedroom.

"Mebbe ah should join ye?" he called to her.

"Aye, maybe ye should," she called back.

He chuckled.

"Ah'll be there in a minute."

He hadn't told her, but a growing sense of dread had been encircling him the last few days. Something was coming. He could feel it, something that wanted to hurt his Catriona.

He didn't need a piece of paper to tell him she was his wife. They were bound, in heart and spirit, and had been since time began.

That's why he knew one thing for sure.

Noo is the time.

He reached behind Catriona's sofa cushions where he'd hidden the ring Sean had given him. So far, he'd had terrible luck giving it to her, but this time *nothing* would stand in his way.

Staring at the golden band in his fingers, he took a few deep breaths, tucked the ring back into the box, and strode into Catriona's bathroom.

He saw her through the shower glass, naked, her head tilted back as she let the water run down her body.

My bonny lass...

He slid out of his clothes and opened the shower door, holding the ring box behind him.

He could feel his heart pounding in his chest.

"Ah hae sometin' fer ye," he said.

"Oh my—I can see that," said Catriona, giggling.

Her amused expression melted into something more akin to concern. She put her hands on his shoulders to peer into his face.

"Are you okay?" she asked. "You look like you're about to cry."

He swallowed as best he could. His throat was dry.

Isn't that funny? Eyes tae wet, throat tae dry...

"Catriona..." he began. The romantic lines he'd been memorizing flew from his brain like a flock of migrating birds.

"Why do you look so serious? What happened?" she asked.

"Nothin'..."

He mentally flipped through the *book* of things he wanted to say to her, but every page had been erased.

Eejit.

"Um..."

Her brow knit. "What's wrong? You're starting to scare me—"

He pulled his hand from behind his back and held up the ring box. It was soaking wet. He hadn't thought about that.

Oh well...

Catriona laughed. "Should I ask where you just pulled that from?"

She paused, gaze locked on the box, her brow knitting faster than a coffee-drinking grandmother.

"Wait, is that—?"

She looked up at him.

T'is time.

He took a deep breath and found room in the small shower to drop to one knee.

"Catriona. Mah love. Would ye marry me?"

They weren't half the words he'd wanted to say, but he hoped they'd get the job done.

Catriona gaped at the ring as if it were the crown jewels.

"Where did you get that?" she asked, her voice dropping to a whisper.

"Sean gave it tae me tae give tae ye."

She plucked the band from its nest, her fingers shaking. "This is the ring Sean gave *his* wife. Your mother."

Broch nodded. "Ah ken."

"This is his most precious thing."

Broch blinked. He was losing the fight against his tears.

"Not his *most* precious thing," he said.

Catriona covered her mouth with her hand. It looked as though she was crying, though it was hard to tell in the running shower.

"Is that an *aye*?" he asked.

"My *Kilty*." She threw her arms around his neck as he stood so their tears could mingle.

"*Yes.*"

CHAPTER TWENTY-NINE

Gog's eyes fluttered open.

He was looking at bar stools tucked beneath what looked like a kitchen countertop.

This doesn't look like prison.

His head felt *cloudy*, like a storm had rolled into the center of his brain. Flashes of lightning. Rain. The whole thing, like the storms he used to watch through the window as a kid.

When the lightning in his head flashed, he saw the guards aiming guns at him. He jerked as the blasts shattered the dull hum in his head.

Pain flared in his chest and under his left eye. He slapped his hand to his face, but it felt normal. No holes where they shouldn't be.

He grunted.

I traveled.

It worked.

He felt a wall against his back and slid up it to his feet.

Now, he could see over the bar. Refrigerator, stove...*not prison.*

He was *hungry*.

Gog took a few wobbly steps to the refrigerator and opened it. Jerking out the lunchmeat drawer, he opened a pack of ham and stuffed the entire wad into his mouth. He found cheese and did the same.

That's when he heard it.

Voices.

He stopped chewing.

A giggle.

A *woman.*

Gog swallowed.

He hadn't touched a woman in three years.

Prison didn't bother him—three squares a day, and a roof over his head was never a bad thing. Prison made as good a place as any to wait for his master's call.

Except for women.

He did miss those.

Following the voices, he walked out of the kitchen and through a doorway into a bedroom.

He blinked at the bed in front of him.

Nice.

Now, he just had to find the woman.

He became aware of a hissing sound. Water? A shower? He spotted another door, mostly closed, on the opposite side of the room.

Bathroom.

She's in the shower.

Even easier—

He took one step before his eye fell to the ground in front of the bathroom door.

A pile of plaid fabric.

A kilt.

Highlander.

It all came back to him. Rune on the television, breaking that kid's throat, the guards shooting, thinking about Los Angeles and the Highlander Rune wanted dead.

His enemy.

He must have jumped right to the Highlander's apartment or, judging by the items in the bedroom, his girlfriend's.

I hope she's young.

Gog looked around the room. Not a bad place to hole up for a couple of days while he looked for Rune.

He couldn't have planned his jump better. He'd bust in and kill the Highlander right in front of his girlfriend.

Then she'd see who the real man was.

CHAPTER THIRTY

Catriona felt Broch's wet body stiffen. They'd been playing, laughing in the en suite shower, he sitting on the built-in bench, she scrubbing his hair with her good nails and his favorite shampoo. She felt the mood shift, and his body went rigid.

"What's wrong?" she asked.

"Somethin's nae richt," he said.

"What do you mean?"

He stood and rinsed the shampoo from his hair. She reached to turn off the water, and he put a hand on hers to stop her. She looked at him, and he shook his head, placing his opposite index finger over his lips to ask for silence.

That's when Catriona realized this wasn't one of Broch's *general* feelings of ill-ease.

Someone's in the house.

She swallowed. This was like a standard reoccurring nightmare. Naked in the shower was the last place she wanted to be in this situation. Her gun was in the closet. Maybe she could get to it—

Broch eased open the glass shower door and stepped out. He held his hand out to her, and she took it, feeling helpless but trusting his instincts.

He set himself up beside the door to the bedroom and ushered her behind him.

They waited.

She had so many questions. Could he *see* who it was? How many people were in the apartment? Did he *know* someone was outside the door? She assumed he did because he'd made no attempt to move into the bedroom.

Adrenaline pumped through her veins until she could feel herself vibrating.

That's when she saw a masculine hand touch the cracked-open bathroom door, fingertips grazing the wood.

It looked *big*.

She saw tattoos on the wrist as the door began to open.

That narrowed things down.

A man, but not Rune. Not Huck. Not Pete making an unannounced visit. This was either a home invasion—which seemed unlikely considering the studio's security—or Rune had found a new thug to send after them the way he'd had Joseph working for him.

If only I could get word to Anne.

She could have Michael zap her right to the apartment—

Broch dropped to a squat.

Wha—?

One moment, Catriona's hands had been resting on his back. The next, her arms dropped. For a split second, she found herself staring at a new face.

A man. She'd known that much. But she'd never imagined the *beast* standing before her. He was tall, taller than Broch, and *big*. Barrel-chested. His head was bald.

At first, she thought it might be Huck's man, Delmont, but this intruder had something Delmont didn't—pointy tattooed teeth encircled his mouth, giving him a demon-like appearance. Two black squares were painted on his forehead. It took a second for her to piece together they were the butt-ends of ram's horns that continued over his ears where she couldn't follow them.

He saw her, and his eyes lit with an emotion she didn't want to investigate.

His gaze dropped to her naked body.

His eyes didn't drop farther than her breasts before Broch, crouched in front of her, slammed his fists into the man's crotch.

The whole introduction took two seconds.

It felt like an *hour*.

With the wind knocked out of him, the demon-man bent forward. Catriona saw the top of his skull, where a single word was tattooed. It was upside down, but it didn't matter. The name Catriona had heard on Huck's show lit up in her mind like a Broadway sign.

Gog.

How Gog had found Rune and gotten his marching instructions so fast she couldn't fathom, but they needed him *gone.*

Broch stood and put his hands on Gog's head. Pressing the sides between his palms, he slammed the man's face into his knee.

Gog twisted, and without hair to help Broch keep his grip, the beast slipped away from him. He lifted an elbow as he moved, catching Broch on the jaw, knocking him to the side.

That's when Broch slipped.

All the Highlander's rage and power were rendered helpless by a pool of water on a tile floor.

Broch fell to the right, crashing into the shower door. For a moment, Catriona thought it would hold, and he would bounce back.

No.

The safety glass shattered into a million spidery pieces. Broch collapsed inside the closet-like structure of the standing shower. His head struck the back wall tiles with a sound that made Catriona's stomach lurch.

She faced forward again, staring into the horrifying visage of Gog. Blood streamed from his nose, covering his lips and chin.

She said the only word in her head.

"*No!*"

She kicked, aiming for his crotch.

She felt her foot slip and her arm thrust out to catch her balance against the wall.

Gog grabbed her wrist and kept her from falling.

She would have rather fallen.

It was too late.

He jerked her toward him, wrapped his arms around her chest, and pulled her naked, struggling body out of the bathroom.

She tried to slam her skull into Gog's chin as he dragged her backward. Broch's body lay half in the shower, half out, still unmoving. She called to him. Screamed his name.

He didn't move.

She writhed, trying to find *any* way to hurt the monster. His arms were like steel bands around her, squeezing the breath from her lungs. The room spun as she struggled for air.

Gog fell forward on the bed with her beneath him. What breath she had remaining burst from her lungs.

I can't black out. I can't.

She knew if she passed out, she'd never wake up.

Or she wouldn't want to.

He squirmed on top of her, trying to pull down the thin prison togs he wore.

The world closed in as if it were being sucked into a pinhole of light.

Then, she heard a horrible *crack.*

Gog's head, positioned above hers, jerked to the left.

Hard.

Fast.

The brute's weight lifted from her chest.

Catriona sucked in a breath as the room came back into focus. A man stood over her.

Not Gog.

Broch.

He stood at the foot of her bed. Naked. Covered in blood. Wet. His straggly hair stuck to his shoulders and cheeks. He looked like a demon lumberjack striding from a dark forest on the edge of hell.

His eyes were wild. He held something white and square with a jagged edge in his hands.

The lid of her toilet tank.

Well, half of it.

She wouldn't have believed there was a sound more sickening than the thud of Broch's head hitting the tiled shower wall until she heard the sound of a large man's skull getting struck by a porcelain lid.

She and Broch stared at each other for a second, and then he was on the move, circling to the other side of the bed. The hunk of porcelain rose into the air and dropped down somewhere below her vision.

A third unimaginably *horrific* noise.

Broch dropped to one knee. Again. This time, instead of asking her to marry him, he was pounding the skull of a man to a pulp.

His face illuminated with a quick flash of light.

He lowered the makeshift weapon.

His shoulders slumped.

"You killed him?" she asked.

"Dead or nearly dead, ah dinnae ken, but he's gone," he said. He dropped the lid and moved to her side on the bed, pulling the covers with him to cover her.

"Are ye hurt?" he asked as he tucked the blanket around her shivering body. The adrenaline dump had her quaking.

She shook her head. "No. Are you okay?"

He nodded and closed his eyes as he pulled her wrapped body against him.

She lay her head on his chest and felt him breathe.

CHAPTER THIRTY-ONE

Huck got out of his car and looked around. No one had followed him.

Good.

He wasn't sure if he was more worried someone would figure out what he was up to or embarrassed to be seen in the squalid neighborhood Rune had picked for his hideout.

He felt like an idiot, but what could he do? Rune was hopeless. Huck had offered to take the creep to Scarpetta for dinner, and *he'd turned him down.*

What moron refuses Scarpetta?

Though, come to think of it, he wasn't sure the ghoul *ate* anything but people. The last thing he wanted was Rune eating his favorite waitress. Her pendulous breasts made every meal a *joy.*

He braced himself for the pandering in his future. He *hated* being scared of Rune, but if there was one thing he knew, it was how to keep the people in power happy and reap the benefits.

That's exactly what he'd do here.

What good were ideals if you were poor? Some people called him spineless, but no one would remember *them.*

They'd remember *him*; rich and famous Huck Carter.

Meeting Rune *had* been humbling. He'd honestly thought *he* was the only one with the ability to influence the people around him for fun and profit. Now, it seemed like there was an endless supply of people like him—Rune, his daughter, the Joseph character who'd been taken out before he had a chance to meet him, this Gog guy, whoever he was—and a whole list of *losers* Rune said Fiona had. Not only that, but Rune was *next level*, what with his turning-people-to-dust thing.

Rune made him look like an amateur.

He had to respect the power.

He imagined *he* was a younger version of Rune. He just hadn't had time to develop the same skillset yet. He had a big advantage over Rune, too—he had television and fans to spread his message.

Rune didn't have any experience with television. But he'd been honing his skills during a time when people were little more than *mud people.*

Maybe not having media had helped Rune develop other skills? Like the way a blind person could hear better than other people?

Maybe that's why *he* couldn't suck people dry.

He'd had it too cushy.

Anyway, they needed to come up with a plan, and here he was, ready to play along for a little longer.

Huck knocked on the door of Rune's humble abode and heard him call for entry. He let himself in and blinked to adjust to the dull light inside. Rune had all the curtains pulled shut and no lights on.

"Why are you living in the dark?" he asked, pulling off his sunglasses before he tripped and bashed his head on a coffee table that should have been burned for kindling in the thirties.

"Someone knocked on the door," said Rune from the chair where he sat.

The only chair not facing the television.

Such a *weirdo.*

"Someone came looking for the owner?"

Huck checked the lounge chair.

The pile of ash remained.

Rune nodded as his gaze shifted somewhere past Huck. Nervous, Huck turned and noticed another pyramid of dust behind him.

"Uh, good job. I *thought* you looked older," he said as he danced away from it.

Rune looked twenty-six or seven now. He still looked strange as hell with those pale eyes and that hawkish nose, but he looked older. Huck could imagine an army respecting him now—he was sufficiently scary.

Speaking of armies...

"Have you heard from Gog yet?" he asked.

Rune frowned. "No. I'm starting—"

A flash of light made them raise their arms to protect their eyes. Huck's anxiety shot to ten. He was sure the LAPD had thrown a flash grenade into the house.

He was about to be gunned down.

Here, of all places.

How would they ever explain finding his body in a shithole—

He stiffened as something close *growled.*

No.

More like a *gurgle.* A guttural gurgle.

He lowered his arms, expecting to see some sort of reptile leaping at his throat.

Nope.

No alligators. Just an enormous man lying on the ground at Rune's feet.

Huck took a step back to be safe. The man lay on his hip, chest twisted toward the ground, head held aloft by a half-pushup, face pointed at the filthy carpet.

The back of the man's bald skull had a word printed on it.

Huck squinted to read it.

Gog.

Hm. That solved one mystery.

Isn't it nice when strangers appear with their names printed on their heads? Saves a lot of boring introductions.

"I'm going to go out on a limb and say this is Gog," said Huck. "*Tada!*"

To be fair, though his tone was mocking, Huck *was* impressed. Gog was the biggest man he'd seen in a long time, and in his line of work, he met a *lot* of goons.

"Gog," said Rune.

Gog moved slowly, turning himself over as if his weight was too much to bear. He inhaled a watery breath.

Huck gasped and slapped his hand over his mouth in horror.

The monster man's face was a mangled *disaster.* For one, he had horns tattooed to his forehead that looped back and around his ears like a ram's rack. Something had been etched on his chin and around his mouth, but it was hard to tell what. *Teeth?* A skeleton-like jawbone decorated the side of his face, so Huck guessed the mess around his lips *were* teeth of some kind, but his face had been—

Huck couldn't think of a better term than *caved-in.*

Was he supposed to look like that? Was he a monster from a time when people didn't have faces?

Huck looked to Rune to take the lead and knew he wasn't alone in his horror. It was clear Rune didn't understand what he was looking at either.

"What happened to you?" asked Rune. He sounded like a disappointed father.

"Kyander," said Gog working his mangled maw. His jaw was certainly broken. Huck nearly tossed his lunch, watching the man try to speak.

"The Highlander did that to you?" asked Rune.

Gog nodded. He seemed in pain. He wheezed, struggling to breathe through his flattened face.

Huck caught Rune's eye. "What the hell is that?" he whispered.

Rune frowned. "The Highlander crushed his face."

"Ya think?"

Rune rolled his eyes. "Wounds received from other travelers don't heal fast. Sometimes, they don't heal at all."

"So he lives like *that* now?"

Gog moaned.

Rune sighed. "You're a disappointment, Gog."

Gog shifted to his knees and bowed as if he were praying to Rune.

"Rune. I am here to serve," he said as red ooze dripped from his face to the carpet. Or he said *something* along those lines. Huck found it hard to tell *what* that mouth full of broken teeth was saying.

Gog made a sobbing sound. He grabbed Rune's ankle, pleading in unintelligible bubbly noises.

Huck squinted to see less.

This is *horrific.*

"I think we're going to have to put him on hold for a few days," suggested Huck.

Gog looked at him.

Huck gagged.

"Maybe a few weeks...?"

Rune shook his head.

He leaned down and wrapped his boney fingers around Gog's arm. Gog straightened, looking as hopeful as a person without a working face could. Rune stroked his gigantic paw once and then gripped it tightly with both hands.

Gog's demeanor changed.

He struggled to pull away, but Rune held him fast with strength Huck hadn't imagined the bag of bones had.

A second later, Gog disappeared into a pile of ash that sprinkled to the ground like the world's most isolated rainstorm.

The whole process had taken five seconds.

Huck gulped as a thimble of spit wedged in his throat.

"You ate him," he said.

Rune looked triumphant. "I didn't know I could do that to other travelers."

Huck shook his head. "Neither did I."

Note to self.

He was counting on that little detail saving his life.

Rune looked at him, his eyes wide.

"The *power*...I can *feel* them. I can *see* them."

Huck was distracted, still pondering the chances of having the life sucked out of him.

"Hm?" he asked.

"I can *feel* them. All of them." Rune stood and stretched his hands out to his sides.

He *glowed.*

Huck took another step back.

What fresh hell is this?

Rune closed his eyes, his chin nodding as if he were watching a procession walk before him.

"No, no, no, no, yes..." he muttered.

His glow faded until it disappeared.

Rune opened his eyes.

"I think I did it," he said.

He looked pleased.

"Did what?"

"I could *always* sense the others when they were *near* me. Fiona gets that from me. But with Gog's power inside me, I can feel them even far away. There was a web—"

"So we have to go get them? A few like Gog only, uh, not so, um...*mushy*?"

Huck realized this conversation was leading toward a road trip with Rune, which sounded like the world's *worst* buddy movie.

He couldn't think of anything worse.

Rune shook his head. "No. *Better.* I called them to *me.*"

Huck's attention returned to the pile of ash that used to be Gog. "Are you sure that's the way to do it? It didn't work out so well with this one."

"Gog went to the Highlander directly, like a *fool.* He was unprepared. I called them to the Yucca brevifolia."

"Yucky *what*?"

"Yucca bevifolia. The park."

"Is that some medieval thing?"

Rune snorted. "Don't be stupid. They're not that old."

Huck gave up. Honestly, he didn't care.

"Uh-huh. Right. Of course not," he muttered, hoping the loon would drop the whole thing.

Rune steadied his freaky gaze on him.

"We should go wait for them. I need you to drive me there and to help me lead them."

Huck nodded.

Finally.

He didn't like the part where he was reduced to chauffeur, but it seemed the recognition he deserved was coming.

"Sure. Whatever you need, boss. I rented a sweet little Porsche Boxster like I used to have in college while I'm in between cars."

Huck followed Rune outside.

"We'll pick up something else at the camping store," said Rune, spotting the Porche.

Huck scowled. "The *what*?"

CHAPTER THIRTY-TWO

Catriona awoke with a gasp. Brochan's arms tightened around her.

"Catriona?"

"I'm fine." She took a few deep breaths. "Just a nightmare."

She didn't want to tell him she'd felt herself waking up and thought she'd find herself dying somewhere with Gog staring down at her. She didn't want to tell him how embarrassed she was that she couldn't stop the monster. She'd always been a fighter—she'd always *assumed* she could find a way out of any situation—that no one could get the best of her. But Gog's strength—she hadn't been able to move. Not even a little. He'd been suffocating her with his weight, immobilizing her—

Broch kissed her.

"That monster knocked me oot," he mumbled into her hair.

She nodded.

"Nae even ah could stop him."

She looked at him.

Did he read my mind?

She bit her lip. "But you *did* stop him."

"Tae late," he said. He gave her another kiss on the head and got out of bed. "Time tae gae. Are ye ready?"

She rolled onto her back, still snuggled in her blankets, and smiled.

"Yeah." She sat up and stared at the pile of glass inside her bathroom door. "Mind if I borrow your shower?"

They gathered at Anne's house and sat outside by the pool with drinks and snacks provided by Anne's assistant, Jeffrey. When he finished serving, he sat and munched along with them. None of this otherworldliness fazed him in the slightest. As long as he'd worked for Anne, he'd probably seen stranger things.

The group included Anne, Con, Fiona, Catriona, Broch, and Sean. Luther had been MIA as of late—busy catching up on the ways of the Angeli.

"I guess Kairos business is beneath Luther now," Catriona teased.

Sean chuckled. "He always was a big shot, but don't worry, I've got him working—" He scowled. "What happened to you?"

Catriona touched her eye where she thought she'd expertly covered a bruise left on her cheek by Gog's manhandling. Normally, she would have told Sean everything, but, this time, she found herself reticent to talk about the night before.

Before she could explain, Anne rushed in, looking flustered.

"Okay, where do we stand?" she asked. She noticed Sean's expression and followed it to Catriona's face. "What happened to you?" she asked.

Catriona sighed.

Here we go. Get it over with.

"Gog popped into my apartment."

Sean's eyes bugged. "What? Who's Gog? Are you okay?"

"Gog was a very large and angry man, *was* being the operative word here. We were, uh, *caught off guard*, but we took care of him. Only thing is, we don't know if we killed him *dead* or only shuffled him out of the deck for a second."

"What do you mean he *popped* into your apartment?" pressed Anne.

"*Literally*. The door was still locked. He wasn't there, and then he was."

Anne looked at Sean. "Sounds like he's got that exact location ability your friends Rune and Huck have."

"Luther did it, too." Sean pointed his eyes to the ceiling and shook his head. "I'm starting to feel like a schmuck. I've been leaving my future to fate for centuries. It never occurred to me I could manipulate where I go."

"Can you practice?" asked Con.

Sean smirked. "I suppose I *could*, but I'd have to kill myself over and over to do it, and somehow I feel like that's never going to make it onto my calendar."

Anne sat. "So Gog is maybe out of the picture for a while?"

"Mebbe," mumbled Broch. "But if he shows his face again, ah'll kill him *proper*."

"What did he look like? So we can keep an eye out for him?" asked Sean.

"Close to seven feet tall, thick-built, bald..." Catriona frowned. "Ever see *The Goonies*? Kind of like the big monster-man in that, if he tattooed demon teeth around his mouth and ram's horns on his head."

"Yikes," muttered Fiona.

Anne agreed with Fiona's sentiment. "What else do we *know*?"

"Huck Carter is working with Rune, but we don't know where either of them is at the moment."

"Not true," said Sean. "I know where both of them are. Maybe."

Catriona sat up. "You do? Where?"

"Luther followed Huck to a house in South L.A. Not his usual haunt. Luther thinks Rune is inside. I'm waiting to hear. It might be our best chance to grab them without witnesses."

Anne touched Catriona's hand to get her attention and then pinched the finger with her engagement ring on it.

"Is that what I think it is?" she asked.

Catriona felt herself blush. "Yep. Last night."

"*Congratulations.*"

"Thank you."

Anne winced. "Sooo, you probably want to be alone with him, but if you have people popping directly into your apartment, you need to stay here for now."

Broch overheard and leaned to whisper in Catriona's other ear.

"Bit ah didnae *pack*."

She guessed he was worried about his shower products. The man was *obsessed*.

"Anne has really good stuff here," she assured him. She patted his knee beneath the table.

It seemed to make him feel better.

They had the perfect relationship—he saved her from evil giants, and she made sure he had expensive shampoo handy.

Totally symbiotic.

She nodded at Anne.

"Understood."

"Good." Anne clapped her hands together. "Okay. So the plan is we stop Rune and Huck first, since they're the ones trying to organize some kind of bad-guy union, and then we'll travel around with Fiona sniffing out the others."

"*Sniffing out*," echoed Fiona, looking nonplussed.

"Like a bloodhound," teased Con.

She side-eyed him.

There was a crackling noise, and Luther appeared, standing on the edge of the pool. He wobbled and then fell into the water.

Catriona barked a laugh. She couldn't help it.

A light flashed in the pool, and Luther appeared again, dry, standing beside the table where the rest of them had gathered.

"Dammit. Sorry," he said, looking flustered.

"What are you doing here?" asked Sean.

Luther's shoulders slumped. "I lost them."

"How?"

The big man looked sheepish. "I tried to pop into the house to confirm Rune was there and maybe listen to what they were up to and..." He paused to grimace at the memory. "... and I went home on accident."

Sean scowled. "*Home*? Your house? I don't understand—"

"My thoughts must have wandered to my *actual* home, and next thing I know, I'm in my living room."

Anne chuckled. When Luther glared at her, she held up a hand.

"Sorry. I've never seen a baby Angelus learning to fly before."

Her comment didn't do anything for Luther's mood. He lifted his hands and let them flop to his sides.

"By the time I figured out how to get back, they were gone. Three piles of ash in there, too. I'm guessing the former occupants."

Sean frowned. "Well, shit, Luther. You were our eyes. The flying thing was supposed to be an *advantage*."

"I know. I know. I'm sorry."

Anne wandered inside to pick up the television remote and rewind Rune's interview.

Catriona joined her.

"What's up?" she asked.

Anne waggled a finger at the screen. "Rune mumbles something here I can't hear, some kind of code or another language—"

"Right. I heard that."

Anne played the moment over a few times. The close captioning didn't register the words—just skipped over his mumbling. Catriona squinted at the television as if it would make her hear better.

"*Yucka the portfolio*?" said Catriona repeating what she heard phonetically.

Anne nodded. "Yeah, that's about as far as I've gotten."

The others began to file in to see if they could be of help.

"You see the real problem here, right?" asked Fiona, handing her empty wine glass to Jeffrey without looking at him.

He frowned and took it to the kitchen to refill it.

"What's that?" asked Catriona.

"He doesn't need Joseph's list anymore. He's recreating it by asking people to go to Huck's site and identify themselves on that form they set up."

Catriona sighed. "I know. They might get *more* this way than Joseph ever dreamed..." She straightened. "Wait. That's how he'll *talk* to them."

"Through the form?" asked Anne.

"Through *email*. He'll have to send out a mass email or text to everyone who wrote in to tell him their next steps."

Fiona nodded. "Right, then he can sort them—sense which are his people and which aren't—something the list and Joseph couldn't do."

"We need to steal *his* list," mumbled Anne.

Catriona turned to Sean. "Do we own Huck's website? When Parasol bought his show, did they get access to his lists and website database?"

He shrugged. "I'll make a call and find out."

Catriona turned to Anne. "The way Michael and Con pop up out of thin air—" She glanced at Luther. "—and I guess you, too, if not so well..."

"Don't make me smack you," muttered Luther.

Catriona grinned and continued, "Could they pop into

wherever Huck's website lives and hack it with their electricity stuff?"

Anne laughed. "For as fancy as they are with their powers, they're shockingly low tech. I can see if Michael has any ideas, though."

Sean lowered his phone. "Looks like Huck has autonomy with his website. We don't have any access to it."

Catriona frowned. "*Shoot.* So all we have to go off of is *Yucky bread and folia*?"

"What's that?" asked Sean.

"Rune mumbles something here." She nodded to Anne, who replayed the moment.

Sean perked. "It sounds like he said *Yucca brevifolia.*"

Catriona blinked at him. "That's a thing?"

Sean nodded. "It's Joshua trees. The Latin name for them."

"It means *little leaf*," said Broch.

Catriona looked at him. "You know Latin?"

He frowned. "I *tellt* ye ah did."

She grunted. "Yeah, but I don't think I *believed* it." She turned to Sean. "How do *you* know this?"

He shrugged. "I have yucca around the house, and I've hiked the park a bunch of times..." He glanced at Broch. "She thinks we're stupid because we're men."

He nodded. "Ah *ken.*"

Catriona ignored them and looked at Anne. "Could he be asking them all to go to Joshua Tree National Park?"

"Maybe. Maybe he accidentally said his plans out loud."

"It's secluded. He could gather a group there without anyone knowing..." said Sean. "The problem is, it's *huge.* He'd have to give them coordinates or something, so they weren't wandering the desert like Moses for weeks."

"So *that's* what's going out in the emails," said Anne. "The coordinates."

Catriona nodded. "We need one of those emails."

Broch shrugged. "Sae fill oot the form. Ye said the people put ye-snails intae the form, and Rune sends them word."

"*Ye-snails*," echoed Catriona, laughing. "That's off, but you're right—we can fill out the form. Rune has no idea who any of these people are—even if they're *us.*"

Sean high-fived Broch.

Catriona scowled. "I'd already said we should—"

"Did ye?" asked Broch.

Sean high-fived him again.

Catriona sighed.

Anne jogged out of the room and returned with a laptop.

"I'll use the email I set up for ordering online. Nothing about it would raise any flags."

"You   mean   it   isn't KairosKiller@AnneBonnyThePirate.com?" asked Catriona.

Anne chuckled as she typed.

"Got it," she said a moment later. "There's an autoresponder with a link to a quiz—questions for weeding people out. Boy, they put some thought into this."

"Well, we should know the answers—or at least Broch, Luther and Sean should."

Anne nodded and read the first question.

"How many times have you been?"

Sean scowled. "What is that? A Buddhist Koan?"

"I guess they mean how many times do you remember existing," said Luther.

The time jumpers mulled the question.

"Ah remember three," said Broch.

"Four for me," said Sean.

"I've got twelve," said Luther.

All eyes turned to him.

He shrugged. "Why do you think I got the pay raise?"

Anne returned her attention to the screen. "Okay. No reason to show off. Let's go with three. Next question. *How did you travel?*"

Sean smiled. "Ah, *tricky.* He's asking how we died."

"Fiona murdered me," said Broch.

Fiona stuck her tongue out at him.

"That's a little personal," said Sean. "Let's go with natural causes, knife, and fall."

Anne typed. "Last one. *What is your life philosophy?*"

"*Survival of the fittest* is his mantra, right?" asked Catriona.

Sean grimaced. "I don't know. It's a little on the nose. They might think we're just parroting what Rune said in that interview."

"Me," said Fiona.

Attention in the room shifted to her as she took a sip of her wine. She smiled back at them.

"He can talk about *survival of the fittest* all he wants, but what it boils down to is *me over you*. Every time. Me, me, *me*."

She took another sip.

"Take it from *me*."

CHAPTER THIRTY-THREE

William Marshal reached behind his back to wrap his fingers around the hilt of his primary broadsword. He always carried two into battle, arranged in a crisscross pattern on his back.

"Could I lend you one of my swords, Sir Richard?" he suggested to the knight standing before him.

Sir Richard looked up from his phone to offer William a withering glance. "For the last time, my name is *Wyatt*. Call me *Wyatt*."

"Whatever name you prefer, Sir Wyatt. Would you like to borrow my sword?"

"*No. Dude.* It's bad enough I have to fight you during the shows. You're a freakin' *spaz*. I don't want to practice during downtime. *Never*. Stop asking."

William frowned and let his gaze sweep the arena. In the stands, the cleaning crew gathered turkey leg bones and napkins, readying for the second seating. He wanted to let Sir Richard's comments go, but for the man's own good, he felt compelled to push his point.

He cleared his throat. "Meaning no disrespect, but I think if you developed additional strength in your—"

"*Dude.* Give it a rest." Wyatt huffed and stormed away to the sound of creaking armor, his gaze still locked on his phone.

William sighed. None of the other knights at Roundtable Entertainment had any *pride*. When he'd stumbled upon the want-ad for knights, he thought he'd finally found his *purpose* in the new time he'd been born. He'd remembered who he was only a few years before and had resumed his training. He knew swordplay wasn't a useful skill in the twenty-first century as it had been in the twelfth century when he was the much respected and much loved first Earl of Pembroke.

He couldn't help honing his skills. Something inside him insisted. He knew he'd need them again someday.

But not against the buffoons of Roundtable Entertainment. *These men aren't true knights.*

The script occasionally called for him to *lose* a battle, but the idea that he, William Marshal, the greatest swordsman of all time, could ever *lose* to one of these slack jawed—

A sudden pain stabbed William's brain, and he dropped to a knee. Groaning, he put a hand on either side of his skull, pushing against it. It felt as though his head would *explode* if he didn't hold it together.

What is this?

The pain eased a notch.

That's when he heard the voice.

I am Rune. I am your master and king in this world. Our time is now. Come to these coordinates immediately.

The voice rattled off a series of numbers, and William etched them in the arena sand with his finger, squinting as the pain throbbed between his temples.

The numbers repeated six or seven times and then stopped. The pain in his head eased.

Expelling a great puff of air, William rocked back to rest his head against the wall of the arena.

Rune.

He'd been drawn to something online about that man—an interview with Huck Carter. He'd planned to research him more fully after his show.

Now, he wouldn't have to.

I have a king again.

Things were falling into place.

William pulled his phone from his pocket and looked up the coordinates.

Somewhere in Joshua Tree National Park.

He'd have to book a flight.

William stood and strode toward the exit, where Sir Wyatt had propped himself against the wall in the tunnel leading away from the arena.

"We're on in twenty minutes—hey, where are you going?" asked Wyatt as William strode passed him.

William stopped.

He knew he wouldn't be returning to Roundtable. Now, he had only two options—he would die fighting for his king, or he would remain with his king to serve for the rest of his days.

Spinning on his heel, he strode back to Wyatt and backhanded him to the ground.

"You're a *disgrace*," he said.

Wyatt blinked up at him, propped on one elbow, the corner of his mouth bleeding.

"What the *hell*, dude?"

William leaned down, holding Wyatt's gaze steady in his own.

"For the last time," he said through gritted teeth. "My name is not *Dude*."

With that, he whirled and left the building.

He took the costume.

He deserved it.

CHAPTER THIRTY-FOUR

Huck slid his credit card from the back of his phone case and swiped it through the checkout at the camping and survivalist supply store where Rune had made him drive.

He didn't like the way things were going.

Not at all.

"Tell me again why we're buying all this crap?" he asked as the girl behind the counter stuffed canteens and rope into a bag.

"We'll need it for the desert," said Rune, putting a trail bar on the pile.

Huck winced. "Yeah, see, I'm not a big camper." He put the trail bar back on the impulse-buy shelf. His card had already been run. No *way* he was waiting for the chick to add that separately.

"We won't be there long," said Rune.

There was no talking to the skinny freak. Huck found himself at a loss. On one hand, Rune was powerful and scared the crap out of him. On the other, sometimes it didn't seem as if he had any idea what he was doing.

Huck had been doing fine on his own. He influenced millions of people from the comfort of his studio. He spun them into frenzies of fear and hate and then toddled off to have a three-star Michelin dinner.

Then Rune waltzes into his life in the guise of his *son*, of all things. This guy thought he could do *better than him* with some ragtag group of losers in the desert.

I doubt it.

Nope. He didn't like the way things were going.

"Get the stuff. We're going this way," said Rune, walking

off without grabbing a single bag.

Huck growled and gathered the bags.

I'm going to kill him.

One more day. He'd follow a little longer to see how things played out at this Burning Man-for-Time-Travelers Rune had planned, but then he'd have to make some decisions.

He paused, realizing Rune hadn't headed for the exit. He'd walked toward the *back* of the store.

Idiot.

The man could reduce people to ash, but he had *no* practical modern-day skills.

I should have sent that kid packing to some Switzerland boarding school when I had the chance.

Huck toted the bags to the back of the store, searching for Rune. Poking his head down a hallway leading toward the rear exit, he spotted a pile of dust.

He sighed.

There he goes again.

I didn't let him have a trail bar, so he ate the manager.

He picked his way around the pile and turned to use his butt to open the back door. The sun blasted at his eyes. He squinted. His sunglasses were on the top of his head, but he didn't have a free hand to pull them down. He was in a sparse parking lot—*employees only,* if he had to guess.

He spotted Rune pointing to a pickup truck with ridiculously large tires.

"This one," said Rune.

"What about it?" asked Huck.

"We're changing cars. We need a truck."

He held up a ring of keys.

Huck scowled. "Any chance those belong to the pile of dust in the hallway?"

Rune continued to hold them aloft until Huck sighed and reached to hook them with the one pinky he had free.

"No, please, don't help," he muttered.

He opened the extended cab and threw the bags into the back as a thought struck him.

"What about the Porche?" he asked. "I can't just *leave* it here."

Rune climbed into the passenger seat. "Leave it. We need a truck where we're going."

Huck sighed again. Ah well. It's a rental. He'd call the

luxury car rental place and tell them to pick the damn thing up if they didn't want their reputation destroyed in front of millions of his viewers.

The truck roared to life, and they drove in silence to a gas station to fill up the nearly empty tank. He donned a cap with the camping store's logo on it that he'd found in the back seat and pulled it low to keep the security cameras from seeing his face.

When they realized the guy from the store was missing, they'd be looking for his *very* identifiable truck.

Huck Carter spotted driving missing man's truck! was not a headline he wanted to see.

He figured if anyone noticed him, he'd say Rune kidnapped him. With his wife and kid missing, people would assume it was part of the same plot. Which, really, it was.

"Fill the canteens as well," commanded Rune in that tone that made Huck want to send him to his room.

Huck went inside the gas station's convenience store with the canteens and came back with six large, bottled waters.

Canteens.

Give me a break.

They continued on to Joshua Tree National Park. Huck tried to pull more information from Rune about where *exactly* they were going and what the hell they were doing, but the skeletal egomaniac wouldn't say a word. He just stared straight ahead with his hands resting on his thighs like the world's ugliest seated mannequin.

"You don't look any older," observed Huck as they entered the park. "I mean, after eating the guy who owns this truck, you didn't age."

Rune sniffed. "I'm old enough."

"So you ate him because—?"

"Because I need his keys."

Huck nodded. "So there's, like, no moral code or *only kill what you need to survive* rule for that power of yours?"

"Turn here," said Rune instead of answering.

Huck slowed and looked out into the desert. Every movie he'd ever seen with guys crawling through the sand dying of thirst flashed before his eyes.

"Are you sure? I don't think you're allowed to leave the path here—"

"Turn. *Go.*"

Rune seemed sure.

Huck checked the gas. He still had more than half a tank.

Fine.

He drove until they came across a sort of natural amphitheater.

Rune pointed, "Park there. This is where we'll wait for them."

"Great," said Huck.

He already regretted removing the trail bar from checkout.

CHAPTER THIRTY-FIVE

A day went by with no word on where to meet Rune. They'd filled out Huck's form and answered the questions multiple times with multiple emails, but nothing telling them specifically where to go ever arrived.

Fiona remained at Anne's house with Catriona, Broch, Con, and Jeffrey. Sean came and went as he tended to Parasol duties.

Fiona talked the group into letting her leave for a few interviews as long as Con accompanied her. They'd had a few 'therapy' sessions—in her car, in her trailer, in a bathroom—just to make sure she didn't revert to being evil again.

You can never be too careful.

Anne checked her laptop for the hundredth time. "What are we missing? Is there some way for Huck and Rune to know which requests are real and which are weirdos?"

Catriona shrugged before turning to catch Fiona's attention. "Could *you* sense who filled out an email form?"

Fiona shook her head. "*I* couldn't, no. But who knows with Dad? I can't turn people to dust, either."

Catriona glanced at her phone. "Sean says Huck's been MIA, so we can assume he and Rune are together. He let the studio know he was taking a sabbatical, and with his wife and kid gone, it's not like anyone can argue with him."

Michael popped into the living room looking dapper as always. He wore a Burberry polo and khakis, his sharp gaze scanning the room as everyone turned their attention to him.

Did he pause a second when he saw me?

Fiona smoothed her hair.

Hello there, sailor.

"I have news," he announced. "We've been sweeping Joshua Tree. There's a steady stream of hikers heading in the same direction—a few desert-appropriate vehicles as well. Two men are waiting there. One is Rune."

"My money's on Huck for the other," said Catriona.

Michael's gaze settled on Fiona. She felt her heart skip a beat.

She tried to look cool.

He stretched out a hand in her direction.

"Come with me. I need you," he said.

"Why do you need *her*?" asked Catriona.

"Mind your own business. The man knows what he's doing," said Fiona, standing.

The Angel crackled with blue light that made the hair on Fiona's arms dance. The room began to fade around her as if a heavy fog had rolled in. The last thing she saw was Con shaking his head as he watched her disappear.

"Every fekkin' time," he said.

Fiona wobbled as she and Michael landed at their destination. She propped her hand on a tall rock beside them and took a moment to focus.

They were in the desert—nothing but sand and scrubby-looking bushes for as far as she could see.

Ick.

Heat radiated from every direction as Michael took her arm to steady her. She abandoned the rock and instead leaned heavily against him with her hand flat on his chest. It made her feel very much like Lois Lane tucking up against Superman.

The Highlander was right.

He does smell amazing.

"Have your feet?" asked Michael.

Fiona realized she was sniffing his neck and peeled herself away from him.

"Hm? Oh, yes. I'm fine. That was quite a ride."

Michael nodded. "It can be disorienting for humans."

Fiona squinted beneath the unrelenting desert sun.

"I don't know if I'm dressed for this," she said as her heels sunk into the sand. She'd remained dressed up on the off chance Michael made an appearance. She'd never dreamed he'd show up to whisk her off to the middle of hell.

Eh. I've had worse first dates.

"You could have told me to bring sunglasses," she scolded.

Michael frowned. "Sorry. Sometimes, I forget human frailties."

She bobbed her head in the direction of the sunglasses on his face.

"Yet, *you* seem prepared?"

He hadn't been wearing those Panthère de Cartiers at Anne's.

He shrugged. "Habit."

"Could I *borrow* them?"

He pulled the glasses from his face and held them out. As soon as he released them into her grasp, they disappeared. She gasped and looked to him for an explanation, only to find the glasses back on his face.

"They're an extension of my energy," he explained, smiling. "They only exist for me."

"Me too," she whispered.

"Hm?"

"Nothing."

The faint sound of laughter reached their ears, and Michael peered around the corner of the rock.

"Your provocative look might come in handy," he said.

She perked. "You think I look provocative?"

His comment pleased her. She'd been going for *readily available* but *provocative* would do.

He ignored her compliment-hunting. "Do you think you could peel that straggler from the pack?"

Fiona peeked out to see who he'd spotted. Far away, three people trudged through the heat towards them—a couple and a third wheel she suspected weighed close to three hundred pounds.

"The *fat* guy?" she asked.

Michael nodded. "He seems to be the odd-man-out. Increases our odds of success."

She arched an eyebrow.

"You don't think I could get between the couple?"

Literally, if that's what you're into, Angelman.

"I'm sure you could," said Michael. "But I'm thinking in the middle of the desert, maybe in the interest of time..."

He looked amused.

Fiona smiled.

Score one for me.

She could tell her charms weren't entirely wasted on the Angel. She was growing on him. Was he her perfect man? Probably not. He was a little *buttoned up*. Was he the best-looking man she'd ever seen? Top five. Did his people *invent* the energy-sipping trick Con used to send her into paroxysms of ecstasy?

Yes, so who cares about the first two things?

"What do you want Chubby for?" she asked.

"I was thinking I could see what effect I have on him."

Her brow knit. "You think he's gay?"

Michael glanced at her, looking confused.

"Hm? *No.* I think *he's* human. I want to know if I can help battle these corrupted Kairos, but I've never hurt a human before—" He paused to cock his head. "Have you ever had a pet that was a total nuisance, but you loved it anyway and knew you could never hurt it?"

She thought for a moment, remembering a Persian with a serious attitude. "I had a cat like that once."

"There you go. Then you know how I feel about people."

"Isn't Anne *people*?"

"Yes. Technically. We enhanced her, of course, but her DNA is human."

"So she's a pain in the ass?"

He laughed. "She'd be the first to admit it."

Fiona realized *Anne* wasn't where she wanted the conversation headed. Sweat beaded on her forehead. Michael looked as if he was sitting in an airconditioned lounge enjoying a scotch on the rocks.

If she was going to make any more progress seducing him, she'd have to hurry before she turned into a raven-haired puddle.

She peeked out at Chubby again.

"So what are you going to try on this guy?" she asked.

"I'm wondering if my electricity could knock him out or disrupt him in such a way it would make Catriona and Anne's job easier."

Fiona wiped beneath her eye to keep her makeup from

raccooning.

"Why don't you just practice on me?"

He considered this. "You? I don't know. For one, these people are different than you. Presumably. I mean, since you've been *cured*."

His stress on the word *cured* sounded judgmental—like she'd had the clap and was fresh off a shot of penicillin.

More like penis-cillin.

She giggled.

"What's funny?" asked Michael.

"Nothing. I crack myself up." She sniffed and stepped back into a spot of shade cast by the rock. "Look, try me. See if you can disrupt me."

"I couldn't—"

"*Try me*, and if it doesn't work, I'll grab the guy for you."

Michael sighed. The group of three had stopped to rifle through their backpacks for drinks, so he stepped into her shady spot, standing very close.

"Okay. I'll try it, but if it hurts, let me know. I don't want to accidentally kill you."

"Maybe just a *little death*," she muttered, tittering to herself.

"What?"

"Nothing.

"Promise you won't let me hurt you?"

She rolled her eyes. "Of *course*. Do you think I'm going to stand here and let you kill me?"

"No. I suppose not—" He seemed to reset himself. "Okay. Just, *anything*—if you feel weak or need me to catch you—"

"Got it."

"Okay, here we go."

He reached up and lightly touched behind her jaw with his fingertips, his pinky brushing her neck.

Oh my God.

Fiona swallowed.

It didn't hurt.

It felt like what Con had done to her.

Oh happy day.

She sucked in an involuntary breath.

Michael jerked his hand from her.

"Are you okay?" he asked.

"Hm? Oh, yeah. I'm *fine*. Continue."

"But you—"

She waved away his concerns. "I'm *fine*. Go ahead."

"Did you feel *anything*?"

"Hm." She shook her head. "Nope..."

He scowled. "Are you sure? I know I pulled energy from you—"

"Nope. Try again. Hurry. They'll be here soon."

Fiona felt like she was going to explode with need. She hadn't been this simultaneously, disgustingly sweaty and aroused since she filmed *Spicy Summer Fling* in Miami with that Spanish actor with the—

Stop.

She had to concentrate. She held her breath, hiding her pleasure. Her legs felt weak.

"Anything?" he asked.

She shook her head.

"Nope," she peeped.

"Are you sure?"

A wave of pleasure overtook her, and her knees buckled. The breath burst from her lungs as she collapsed, panting, into his arms.

"Are you okay?" He scooped her up and draped her over his forearms as if she weighed no more than a tissue.

I think I love this man.

She kept her eyes closed, savoring every last throe of ecstasy.

"You look pained. Did it hurt you?" he asked. "Should we go back?"

She reached up and gripped his upper arm. "*No.* No. I'm good. Give me a second."

"So I *did* incapacitate you?" he asked.

"Oh yeah," she said. "*Definitely.*"

He fell silent. When she opened her eyes, he was staring down at her, a disapproving glare on his face.

"What?" she asked.

He let her feet drop to the ground.

"It didn't hurt," he said.

It wasn't a question this time.

She hemmed. "A *little*—"

"*It didn't hurt,*" he repeated.

She smirked. "No."

He huffed. "Dammit. I knew it and—"

She perked. "You knew it? And you didn't stop?"

"I meant, I had a *feeling*—"

"You have feelings?"

"*Fiona*," Michael hissed through clenched teeth. "Stop twisting my words."

She laughed. "You are *adorable* when you're flustered."

He grimaced.

Pouted, really.

"I won't tell Anne. It'll be our secret," she promised.

"I didn't do anything *wrong*," he said and then rushed to qualify his statement. "Anne and I aren't—"

Fiona's eyes widened. "Dating?"

"No, we—" He sighed. "When you're immortal, or in her case, *practically* immortal, monogamy is a bit much for anyone. We're *fluid*. Right now, we're on. Sometimes we're off."

"That's when she's with Con?"

Michael grunted.

Before she could investigate when he and Anne might be taking their next *break*, voices lilted through the air again, much closer this time.

Michael straightened. "Oh thank God. Let's get back to work."

She looked at him. "You still want to practice on this guy?"

"No, but I want to see if you can sense if they're Kairos."

She shrugged. "Easy enough."

The two of them stepped out from their hiding place. Startled, the group stopped fifteen feet away.

Fiona considered them as they stared back at her. She pointed—girl, boy, third wheel.

"Yes, no, yes."

"You're sure?" asked Michael.

"I'm sure." She motioned to the girl. "She brought him for protection and, um, camping prowess. She hasn't told him the real reason she's here because she's a stone-cold bitch."

"*Hey*," said the girl, scowling.

"You can read their minds?" asked Michael.

Fiona shook her head. "No. It just doesn't take a genius to figure a girl might want to bring a guy to protect her when she wanders into the desert."

"You're saying he's not one of us?" asked Chubby. He glared

at the young man.

"Back off, fatboy," said the jock.

Chubby pulled an angry-looking knife from his belt. "You're not one of *us*," he said, waggling it.

Michael rolled his eyes.

"Give me the knife," he commanded.

The big guy scowled. "Who the hell are you to tell me what to do?"

Fiona heard a crackling sound and scurried back, tripping in the soft sand. She fell to her tush, watching as Michael levitated a foot off the ground. A moment later, he unfurled what looked like wings made of blue lightning from his back.

Her jaw creaked open and hung like that.

He's the most beautiful thing I've ever seen.

The three travelers gaped at the Angel, stumbling back in their fear. The tip of Michael's wing shot forward to envelop the knife, jerking it from the man's grasp.

Chubby fell back onto the sand. The girl screamed.

"Nobody hurts anyone. Do you hear me?" boomed Michael.

The three nodded, their eyes wide with fear.

Michael held a hand out to Fiona, and she stood to take it without question.

"Let's go," he said.

The fog rolled in again, and the desert faded from view.

CHAPTER THIRTY-SIX

Jeffrey chopped vegetables at a steady pace as Anne stuck her head in the refrigerator in search of something to nibble. She spotted a package of lunchmeat and pulled it out as the familiar crackling sound of a visiting Angelus filled the air.

"Oh good, yer back," said Con, flatly, from his perch on the sofa.

Anne looked up to see Michael and Fiona standing in the living room. Fiona looked like a drowned rat.

"Hot there?" asked Anne.

Fiona narrowed her eyes. "Little bit."

"Here's the plan," said Michael, ignoring Con and getting right down to business, as usual. "The crowd has gathered. I'd estimate thirty, forty tops. There are some stragglers and some regular humans brought as companions, so we can't go scorched earth."

Anne bit into the chunk of sliced ham she'd rolled into a tube and considered this information.

"Do we know if we'd hurt the humans if we siphoned them by accident?"

Michael shook his head. "No. We don't know."

Anne threw back her head. "Catriona!"

"Jeez," said Jeffrey, shuddering. "I'm using a knife over here. How about a heads up before this quiche is half carrots, half fingers?"

Anne smiled at him. "Sorry."

After a brief delay, Catriona entered from outside, where she'd been sitting by the pool. Her shadow, Broch, followed in her wake.

"We have to test if what we do hurts normal humans," said Anne.

Jeffrey's staccato cutting noises stopped.

"Oh no."

Anne put a hand around his shoulder. "Can we borrow you for a second?"

He grimaced. "I knew it."

"Sorry. You're the only normal human being here."

He sighed. "There's no arguing with that."

"Stick out your arm."

With a huff, Jeffrey held out his right hand and turned his head.

"Be gentle."

Anne and Catriona gripped his arm and, on the count of three, attempted to reboot him. He whined, and they stopped.

"It hurts?" asked Anne.

He blinked at them, grimacing. "Not exactly, but it's *unpleasant.*"

"There's something else to consider—trying to drain humans is a time suck," said Catriona. "We'd be wasting time while the real bad guys were getting away."

Anne nodded. "True. So we *do* need Fiona to identify them before you and I snuff them out."

"Am I done?" asked Jeffrey.

Anne nodded, and he returned to his cooking, grumbling something about poison.

Michael crossed his arms against his chest. "I tested a theory, and I can confirm that myself and the rest of the Angeli won't be much help. It's against our ability to harm humans—even if they're corrupted Kairos."

"It's true. We tried," said Fiona sending a coy look in Michael's direction.

Anne scowled.

What was that about?

Michael noticed Fiona's attention. His cheeks flushed with color. "Um...what was I saying?"

"Ye were sayin' yer useless," said Con without removing the glare he had pointed at Fiona.

Anne assumed Con had caught Fiona's flirty look, too.

So, I'm not crazy.

Fiona sat there with a strange, dreamy smile on her face.

Hm.

"Hey, what about Con?" asked Catriona, oblivious to the drama. "He cured Fiona—can he help us cure the others?"

"I have a hypothesis on that," said Michael. He seemed eager to change the subject. "I don't think Fiona was ever corrupted like Rune and Huck. I think Rune tried to *turn* her— trained her to mimic his instincts, maybe shared a portion of his corrupted energy with her—but it never really *took*."

He looked pleased with himself as he shared his theory. He had an athlete's body and a suave demeanor, but at his core, he was a total nerd.

Fiona animated. "You don't think I was ever sick?"

Michael shook his head. "No."

She turned to stick her tongue out at Catriona. "See? I'm just as good as you. I was just favored by the wrong parent."

Catriona nodded. "Great. Good for you." She returned her attention to Michael. "So you don't think Con can cure them alone? Fiona was an anomaly?"

Con laughed. "Have you forgotten *how* I cured her? I can't line these people up outside my bedroom door—" He reconsidered. "*Though* maybe *some* of them, if you gave me a peek at the ladies. The men are on their own."

"*Animal*," muttered Michael, then louder, added, "I'm confident Con will be of little help."

"I can still fight," said Con. "I'll help more than you will, ya perfumed—"

"*Och*," said Broch, holding up a hand. "There's na getting aroond the fact he smells lik' an *angel*." He turned to Michael. "Ah've been meanin' tae ask ye whit shampoo ye use?"

Michael blinked at him. "I naturally manifest my human form as perfectly groomed, but today I based the scent of my hair on Oribe shampoo. I'll have a bottle sent to you."

"T'is lovely," said Broch. "Ta."

"You're welcome."

Michael looked pleased.

"If he sends you a bottle, don't get used to it," muttered Catriona.

Anne poked Michael's arm.

"Hey, Pretty Boy, can you give us an update on the situation? Maybe we could swap shampoo tips later?"

Con held out a hand to her. "*Thank you*."

Michael nodded. "Yes, yes. Most of the group has gathered

in a natural amphitheater where Rune awaits, but there are stragglers still making the trek. The most logical plan would be for me to transport Anne and Catriona there, pick off the stragglers, and then we'll start on the core group."

"Maybe wait until they disperse and pick them off as they straggle *back*?" suggested Catriona.

"Maybe. Though it might not be wise to wait and let Rune have his meeting. He might be weaponizing them somehow, making them stronger, I don't know."

"Speaking of which, shouldn't we be headed straight for him and worry about the peons later?' asked Anne.

"It might be difficult to reach him with a crowd of adoring fans around him." Michael ran his hand through his hair. "We're going to have to play some things by ear."

"What about me?" asked Fiona.

He eyed her. "I'm going to drop you off with the main group. You can start marking which are normal humans and which are Kairos."

Fiona scowled. "Marking them? You mean literally? How?"

Michael shrugged. "Spray paint?"

"You want to drop me into the middle of an angry mob so I can start *spray-painting* people?"

"I'll go with her," offered Con as he stood. "I'm long overdue for a good scrap."

Michael nodded. "I'm going to take Catriona and Anne to the stragglers. I'll be back to pick you up."

"Can't Con take her?" asked Catriona. "He does that popping in and out thing you do."

Michael shook his head. "He isn't strong enough to carry another person with him."

Con scowled.

CHAPTER THIRTY-SEVEN

As Michael laid out his plans, Catriona noticed Broch's attention jerk toward the Angel.

"Take me wit them," he said.

Michael shook his head. "Just the girls this time. I can only transport so many people, and this should be a breeze."

Broch tensed. "Nah. Ah stay wit' her."

Michael shook his head. "I'll bring you for the main event. I promise."

Broch's jaw clenched.

Catriona thought it might be time to step in. "Broch—"

He turned to her. "Could ah speak tae ye fer a moment?"

"Sure." He strode outside and Catriona followed. He led her around the corner of the house, out of sight from the others, and locked on her gaze with his fiery hazel eyes.

"Ah'm nae leavin' ye," he said.

She put a hand on his arm. "It's okay. I'll have Anne and Michael with me. Michael can whisk me away if anything goes wrong."

Broch's mouth pulled to the side, and he shook his head until his locks bounced on his shoulders.

"Ye dinnae understand." He cupped the side of her jaw in his hand. "Nae one kin protect ye lik' ah kin."

She smiled. "I have no doubt that's true, but you heard him. This will be a *breeze*. It's more a practice run than anything. These are just random people, not trained killers."

"Howfur dae ye ken?"

She cocked her head. "I guess I don't, but I *suspect*. It's not like all these Kairos have been training for this moment. Look at Fiona. If she got into a fight, she'd shatter into a million pieces."

"She's deadly in her way," muttered Broch.

He closed his eyes and took a deep breath. When he opened them, he seemed calmer.

"Fine," he said softly.

He wrapped his arms around her and pulled her tight against his body, his cheek resting against the top of her head.

"Sae yer goan tae marry me after this, richt?"

Catriona smiled. "Do I have to?"

"Aye, ye have tae." He held her at arm's length to look into her face, and his expression relaxed as he saw she was kidding. "Ye already bewitched me intae yer kip, ye siren."

"Do you regret it?" she teased. She reached behind him to put a hand under his butt cheek and pull her pelvis against his.

He grunted. "Yer a witch. That's all ah ken."

He kissed her, his lips lingering, their bodies pressed together.

"Ah loove ye, Catriona Phoenix. Ah want ye tae ken if yer tekkin' from me, ah'll find ye."

"I'm not going anywhere. You know why?"

"Why?"

"Because I looove ye," she said, imitating his brogue.

He laughed.

"Yer a nutter."

She turned to head back to the house, giggling as he slapped her rear.

Like a schoolgirl.

It was *wonderful*.

Catriona threw out her hands to catch her balance as Michael transported her and Anne to the desert. The experience felt a little like being blindfolded and spun for a child's game.

"*Whoa.*"

"It takes some getting used to," said Anne.

When Catriona could focus again, she found herself staring at a group of three—a young man and woman who looked like a couple and a larger man walking behind him.

The group stopped.

"Not again," said the portly one.

"Remember me?" asked Michael.

They turned to run away, and his electric blue wings crackled. He zipped forward, snatched the young man off the ground, and disappeared.

The girl screamed.

"That one was a regular human," said Catriona.

Anne looked at her. "You could tell?"

She nodded, and then her eyes widened.

"Oh my God, I think I *can* tell."

She could barely hear herself. The girl was still screaming.

"Okay. *That* needs to stop," said Anne.

The two of them ran at the girl. Screaming even louder, she threw up her hands and fell on her hip. Catriona and Anne grabbed her flailing arms, one each. They siphoned her until she popped out of their time.

Catriona straightened and took a moment to enjoy the silence.

"That's better."

Her attention moved to the chubby guy, who stood fifteen feet away, his eyes bugging.

"Oh shit," he said when he realized they were looking at him.

He lumbered in the direction from which he'd come.

Anne pat Catriona on the shoulder.

"I got this one. Take your time."

She ran after him with her enhanced speed, easily making up ground on the soft sand. When she was close to him, she thrust out her glowing sword. It sank into the back of his skull.

Catriona winced.

Ouch.

The man's body shook as if he'd been electrocuted. He collapsed to the ground.

"Where can I get one of those?" asked Catriona as she arrived beside Anne.

The two of them crouched to siphon their quarry, and a moment later, he'd *poofed* as well.

"Two down, infinity to go," said Catriona.

Michael reappeared. "All finished?"

Catriona nodded. "Where'd you take the normie?"

"Back to the parking lot."

"What happens when he calls the police?"

"He won't. I wiped his memory."

"You can do that?"

He nodded. "It's a necessary skill we've developed. We have to, or the tabloids fill with angel sightings." He cocked an eyebrow at Catriona. "You *knew* he was a normal human?"

She nodded. "I'm starting to realize the Kairos have a sort of shimmer around them."

Anne slapped her on the back. "Turns out she can do what Fiona does. Must be in the family."

Michael grew pensive. "Handy, though I still have plans for your sister."

Anne frowned. "Yeah, about her—"

Michael seemed to snap to. "We better hurry," he said, rushing to cut her short. He jerked a thumb behind him. "I saw two other groups of stragglers. We'll get them and then move on to phase two."

Catriona smiled. "Sounds like a plan."

CHAPTER THIRTY-EIGHT

This is *ridiculous*," said Fiona, smiling and nodding at a man in the crowd. She could tell he was trying to place why she seemed familiar to him.

"You're almost done. Keep it up," said Con.

Fiona pulled another sticker off the sheet Michael had given her and placed it on the back of a girl under the guise of nudging her out of the way.

There weren't many humans in the crowd, and she was tired of being jostled in the heat.

She glanced toward the curved rock in front of the gathering. Rune was there, sitting on a camping chair with Huck hovering nearby. A large man dressed like a knight stood in front of them with his hands crossed in front of him like a bouncer.

"That man is wearing a suit of armor in the desert," said Fiona.

"I saw that," said Con. "He's Rune's heavy. I'd go wreck him, but the Angel said to stay hidden."

Fiona snorted a laugh. "Since when do you listen to Michael?"

Con shrugged. "Believe it or not, I've spent almost three hundred years doing the bidding of Angeli. Doesn't mean I have to like them."

"Three hundred years, huh? What were you in your first life?"

He bobbed one shoulder. "A pirate."

"Really?" She squinted at him. "*No*. Anne was a real pirate. I suspect you were a petty thief, a rogue, and a man-whore."

He nodded. "That, too."

A man in the crowd locked on Fiona. She watched him start working his way toward her. She pulled her ballcap down to cover her face.

"I'm too famous for this," she muttered to Con as she slapped a sticker on the shoulder blade of a middle-aged man.

The man she'd been watching was nearly upon them.

"Aren't you Fiona Duffy?" he asked as he closed in. It seemed he had no intention of stopping.

Con stepped in front of her.

"Easy, *boyo*," he said, putting a palm in the center of the man's chest.

The man scowled at him.

"I want to talk to Fiona."

Con shook his head. "Yeah, well, she doesn't want to talk to you."

The man was hard. He leaned in.

"How do you know what she wants, asshole?"

Without hesitation, Con punched him squarely in the face. Fiona heard his nose break and turned away to keep from retching.

A ripple of yelps erupted from the surrounding crowd as the rabid fan fell flat on his back like a plank of wood.

Worried the commotion would catch Rune's attention, Fiona glanced toward the rock amphitheater. Rune had stood from his chair and was craning his neck, trying to see into the crowd.

"Good job laying low," hissed Fiona. She grabbed Con's arm and pulled him toward the back of the crowd.

She led him behind a truck with giant monster tires.

"I thought you couldn't hurt humans?"

Con grinned. "That's the Angeli. I can smack 'em around all I like."

She wiped the sweat from her brow with the back of her hand. "We're done. I might have missed one, but I don't think so."

Michael appeared beside them.

"Was that commotion *you*?" he asked.

"No. Nah. Somebody fainted," said Con, hanging his thumbs in his waistband.

Fiona squinted at him.

The man lied like he breathed.

Kinda hot.

She always did have bad boy issues.

"You're finished?" asked Michael.

Fiona nodded. "What now?"

"Now, something all at once. Watch."

He motioned in the direction of the crowd, and Fiona peered around the truck.

As if Michael had given a silent command, a smattering of people in the crowd glowed blue and then disappeared, lessening the crowd by a dozen or so.

"What happened?" asked Fiona as a ripple of excited noise ran through the crowd. Somewhere a woman screamed. Someone yelled, *Dina!* over and over.

"I had Angeli transport the humans to the parking lot all at once. One at a time would have caused a growing confusion—now we can strike while they try and piece together what happened. Anne and Catriona are over there, ready to start."

Rune edged toward the crowd, looking as confused as his minions.

"How do we strike?" asked Fiona.

"You don't. I'm running you home. Anne and Catriona will take it from here."

Fiona huffed a sigh.

"Thank God."

CHAPTER THIRTY-NINE

"What is going on?" asked Huck, scanning the crowd.

They'd been about to address the crowd, and then, all of a sudden, people started *panicking*. Not a little. A *lot*. Everywhere Rune's followers were flailing, screaming, running—

"They're here," said Rune.

Huck turned to him. "Who's here? Is this supposed to happen this way?"

"Protect me," said Rune to the knight standing at his side.

Huck watched as the knight drew his sword.

Then there was that.

The knight.

Huck still couldn't believe it. Everything just got weirder and weirder with this guy.

He was *over* it. Tired of being hot. Tired of being covered in dirt. Tired of playing second fiddle to a full-blown *freak*.

He turned to see if Rune was watching him and saw ol' bag o' bones step into the crowd.

What is he doing—?

Rune grabbed a girl by the throat with such savagery it made Huck suck in a breath.

"*Wha*—Isn't she one of ours?"

Rune heard him. "I need the power again," he said as the girl burst into ash. "I need to reconnect to the web."

"The *web*?" Huck's voice cracked. "We don't even have a *computer*."

Rune moved on, trying to grab another girl who jerked away from him and ran.

Huck twisted, looking for a way out. All around him, it seemed like people were *disappearing*.

At the edge of the crowd, he spotted a familiar face.
Catriona.
Then his gaze settled on the man standing near her.
The Highlander.
"Oh, *hell* no," he said aloud.
Rune didn't hear him. He was trying to catch another victim, but people ran from him. They'd seen what he'd done to the first girl.
Good.
Screw him.
Huck needed to get back to the truck, and he had no intention of taking Rune with him. It was a *miracle* the freak hadn't already sucked *him* to ash.
"F this. I'm out."
The knight looked at him.
Huck pointed toward Rune. "Watch it! That guy's coming at him!"
The knight turned to look, and Huck skittered by him.
Forget Rune.
Forget his plans for world domination.
Forget his freaky blue eyes and stupid ideas.
He was going to get as far away as possible, have a long shower, and have a good meal.
Maybe Scarpetta.
Then he'd get back to taking care of Number One.
Me.

CHAPTER FORTY

Anne and Catriona scanned the crowd as the Angeli whisked away the regular humans.

"Didn't thin out the crowd much," said Catriona.

Anne sighed. At least, Catriona *thought* she sighed—she saw the pirate's chest rise and fall, but she couldn't hear the sound as the crowd reacted to the disappearances with screams and frantic calls.

"Incoming," said Anne.

Catriona turned in time to see a girl headed their way. She stuck out a leg. The girl tripped hard and slid into an imaginary second base.

Like synchronized swimmers, Catriona and Anne dipped to grab her exposed calf.

The girl yipped once, made a quick and failed attempt to scuttle away, and then disappeared.

"One down, thirty or so to go," said Anne.

Michael appeared with Broch by his side. He'd changed into his kilt.

Not a shocker.

"You're here in full costume," said Anne.

"Ah wouldnae miss it fer the world," said Broch, sticking out an arm to clothesline a man running past him. The man's feet flew into the air, and he hit the ground with an explosion of breath. Catriona and Anne made short work of him.

Anne clapped her hands together. "Okay, we've got to hurry. They're getting away."

She was right. Some of the panicked Kairos had headed back down the path toward the parking lot.

"I can help you with that," said Michael, motioning toward

a man who'd made it twenty yards away from the core group. Though Michael didn't move, the running man flashed with blue light and then appeared a foot away from them.

Catriona and Anne lunged forward and drained him while he was still disoriented.

"What was that?" asked Catriona.

"I have Angeli stationed around the perimeter. We might not be able to hurt humans, but we can transport them back here when they try to get away."

"*Perfect*," said Anne, thrusting her sword into the head of a passing young man. He shuddered and dropped to his knees, where she and Catriona grabbed him.

New screams erupted from somewhere near the front of the remaining crowd. Catriona strained to see. A man moved out of her field of vision to reveal Rune wading into the crowd to grab a girl by the throat.

She watched as the struggling girl burst into ash.

Catriona gasped.

"He's killing them." She turned to Anne. "He's draining his own people. Why would he do that?"

Anne shrugged and plunged her sword into the chest of a middle-aged woman.

"I don't know, but he's only helping us."

No sooner had Catriona helped her drain the woman than a man nearby locked on her and threw back his head, roaring.

"Oh boy, we've got a live one," she said. He ran at her like a charging rhino. When he was close enough, she side-kicked him in the mid-section, and he doubled over. He stumbled forward another step in that bent position, and Catriona elbowed the back of his neck to knock him to the ground. Anne put a hand below his skull to hold him to the ground, and Catriona dipped to complete their connection. He disappeared.

Catriona spotted Broch in a fistfight with another big boy. She pointed him out to Anne, who ran over to stick her sword into the attacker's back. He straightened like a puppet who'd had his strings yanked. Broch knocked him cold with a right cross, and the girls took care of him.

"Ah had him," said Broch sheepishly.

Catriona patted his arm and smiled. "I know." She backhanded a blond trying to swing on her, and Broch held the girl until Anne could join for the finale.

"Look," said Anne, pointing into the crowd. A collection of bodies were lying in the sand toward the back of the pack.

Catriona scowled. "What happened to them? Did Rune do that, too?"

"*There*," said Anne pointing to her left.

Con was in the crowd, knocking out people at a terrifying pace. One punch, and they fell like sacks of grain.

"That's his thing. Punching," said Anne.

Catriona whistled. "I can see that."

Anne and Catriona jogged over to siphon Con's victims where they fell. They were able to sweep up eight Kairos in two minutes.

"Nice job," said Catriona.

Con grinned, panting from the effort of punching so many faces. "Figured it would be easier for you if they were unconscious."

Catriona turned to offer the idea to Broch. With Con *and* Kilty smacking people unconscious, they might be able to sweep up the rest of the crowd in record time.

"Hey—"

He wasn't behind her anymore. She made a three-sixty sweep, scanning the crowd.

Broch was gone.

CHAPTER FORTY-ONE

The desert dust devils had filled the air with ash.

Broch felt the knight before he saw him.

Anne and Catriona were busy siphoning Con's casualties. Distracted, they didn't know what was coming.

Broch turned to see the knight striding toward him. The man held a broad sword in his hand. The people in the crowd, still struggling to understand who or what was attacking them, scrambled to make way for him.

He wore a suit of armor and was headed straight for Catriona.

Broch moved to intercept him.

"Whofur are ye?" he asked, putting himself in the man's path.

The knight stopped and eyed his kilt.

"You're the Highlander? The one my lord spoke of?"

"Ah am. Whofur are ye?"

The man pounded the hand holding his sword against his chest. "I am William Marshal, the greatest swordsman who has ever lived."

Broch smirked. "Ye dinnae say."

He fought to keep his scornful sneer from dying on his lips as memories were triggered. Something about the man's name reminded him of his lessons as a young man—lessons about a knight from the thirteenth century by the name of William Marshal.

The greatest swordsman in history.

Could it be?

Was this man the same knight? Or was he a buffoon

playing dress-up?

Either way, the man had an advantage with that hefty sword in his hand. William wouldn't need to be the greatest swordsman of all time to get the drop on an unarmed Highlander.

Ah should hae brought a sword.

Broch cursed his poor planning. He thought he'd be doing little more than holding people in place while Anne and Catriona siphoned them. Maybe, with some luck, he'd get the opportunity to break Rune's scrawny neck, a pleasure he'd been dreaming about for centuries.

He wanted to do that with his bare hands.

Now, it seemed he'd underestimated his foes.

William Marshal held his gaze while Broch strained to find a clear path to victory. After a measured moment, the knight reached behind his back and pulled a second sword from a scabbard strapped on there. Flipping it, he held the blade out to him.

"I'll defeat you honorably," he said.

Broch blinked at the sword.

A trick?

No.

The knight seemed sincere.

Broch took the sword and tested its balance.

"T'is a fine blade," he said.

William seemed pleased. "I had them specially made for me."

The knight took a fighting stance.

"Good luck to you, Highlander."

Broch squared with him.

"Na offense, bit ah'm hoping ye lose."

William slashed at him, and Broch dodged back, the blade barely missing his arm.

He charged forward. Their steel met with a clanging of metal. Broch could tell by the exchange that William was no fool pretending to be the famous knight. He shuffled back a step to give himself additional reaction time.

William came at him like a hurricane. He knocked Broch's sword aside and cut the meat above his hip. Broch roared and continued forward, spinning past the knight, narrowly missing a second wound as William's blade cut through the air beside him.

"You may kneel, and I'll end this for you quickly," offered William.

Broch swallowed. He was a *good* swordsman, but it appeared he was better at making swords than he was at fighting with them.

William fought at a different level.

The knight glanced over his shoulder, keeping an eye on the whereabouts of Catriona.

Broch's jaw flexed. He lunged forward to take advantage of the man's distraction.

He realized too late it had been a ruse.

The knight met his blade with his own. Only Broch's strength kept William's sword from splitting his skull.

Though he hadn't been wounded in this most recent exchange, the damage had been done. The warriors were close now, wrists so tight it looked as if they were bound together.

Too close.

From nowhere, a dagger appeared in William's free hand.

He plunged it into Broch's stomach.

The Highlander hung there, frozen, straining to keep the larger blade from taking his head.

William could have stabbed a second and a third time, but he didn't.

He didn't need to. His first strike had been well placed.

The knight released him and stepped back, leaving the dagger embedded. Without resistance to hold him upright, Broch dropped to his knees.

The sword fell from his hand to the rough desert landscape.

William bent to retrieve his spare blade.

"You were a fine opponent," he said, wagging a finger at him. "But you should have taken my offer. *That* wound will provide you a slow and painful death."

As the taste of blood filled Broch's mouth, the knight returned the second sword to his back and strode away.

Broch watched him go.

William was headed toward Catriona, his primary blade still in his hand.

On his knees, Broch reached forward, clawing at the air. He tried to call out, offer some warning, but no voice came.

No.

He saw Catriona ahead. Her back was turned to the knight. She didn't know he was coming.

No.

He struggled to find his feet as the tip of William's sword raised, preparing to run Catriona through.

Broch grit his teeth and strained to rise. One foot found the earth. He balanced on one knee as he gasped for breath, coughing blood, the pain in his stomach radiating.

He knew his progress was too slow. He'd never find the strength to run after William. Even if he could, he wouldn't have the power to stop him. He'd been rendered weaponless once again—

He looked down.

The hilt of William's dagger protruded from his belly.

He was dying. He could feel it. Removing the weapon would quicken his bleeding.

His fingers brushed the hilt.

He felt his life slipping away. It would be a risk, but a risk he had to take.

There was no other way.

He gripped the dagger.

This is goan tae hurt.

CHAPTER FORTY-TWO

Catriona turned in time to see a man striding towards her.

A knight?

She had no time for another thought or reaction. The knight was upon her, the sword in his hand aimed at her heart.

She didn't have the time to move.

She winced as the blade glided forward, bracing for an end she couldn't prevent.

No pain came.

Catriona opened her eyes.

The knight was gone.

No, not *gone*—invisible to her. Her view had been blocked by a broad back in a bloodied white shirt.

A man wearing a kilt.

Broch.

He'd appeared from nowhere.

He had even less time to react.

The knight's blade ran through the Highlander, even as Broch slashed the knight's throat with the dagger in his hand.

Blood sprayed.

The knight retracted his blade as he reached to stop the river of red gushing from his throat. His knees buckled, but before he could hit the ground, he disappeared.

Broch remained. He dropped his dagger and collapsed to the ground.

"*Broch!*"

Catriona fell to her knees beside her fallen Highlander.

"I have to stop the blood," she told him, pushing him from his side to his back.

He groaned as he rolled. "It's a mortal wound, lass."

She shook her head. "No. No, it's not. You're strong. We can fix it. Medicine is so much better—"

He reached up to touch her face. "Who's goan tae protect ye?" he asked, his voice weak.

Broch's eyes welled with tears.

She set her jaw. "*You* are. Broch, don't—"

"I'll find ye," he said, his eyes closing.

"*No*—Broch!"

Catriona fought to see through her tears. She pressed her lips against his, kissing him everywhere she could reach—his lips, his cheek, his forehead.

Between kisses, she begged.

"Wake up. Wake up for me, Broch. Don't leave me. *Please* don't leave me."

Her heart ached, filling her chest with pain, choking her.

"Broch—"

He shimmered.

"No!"

Then he was gone.

She gaped at her empty hands, horrified.

"No! *No!*"

She stood, spinning, looking for him to appear again nearby.

"Broch!"

Anne approached. She'd seen everything.

"Catriona, I'm so sorry—"

"No, no...he'll be back. He's here. He has to be—"

Catriona stopped spinning.

Anne's voice faded into the distance.

That's when she saw him.

Huck.

The weasel was scurrying away. Rage burned in her like an all-consuming flame.

"*You*," she said, clenching her teeth so hard she thought they might crack.

"Huck!"

Huck turned. He saw her. He tried to break into a sprint but tripped on the uneven ground. By the time he'd scrambled to his feet, she was on him, kicking out the back of his knees, so he hit the dirt a second time.

She pounced on him.

"Get off of me, you crazy bitch," he screamed, thrashing. "I didn't *do* anything. It wasn't *me*."

Her anger burned.

The lies.

She couldn't take the lies anymore. She punched his stupid face. Over and over, left, then right, as he did his best to block her blows, failing almost every time.

"You piece of *shit*," she screamed at him.

"You're going to go to jail," he sputtered. "You can't do this. You can't kill me."

She grabbed his wrists and, straddling his waist, slammed his hands to the ground on either side of his head.

She wanted to *destroy* him.

He didn't deserve to live.

He'd helped ruin her life. He and Rune had taken the only man she'd ever loved from her.

Her nose hovered inches above his, his face so bloody now he could have been anyone.

She screamed into his face. Roared with all the frustration and hurt and anger inside her.

That's when she felt it.

Huck's life was sucking into her.

She felt her power growing.

Huck went ashen. He howled as if he were being burned by holy fire. His puffy cheeks sank beneath the sheen of blood covering them.

"Catriona!"

She heard the voice behind her. Orange light glowed in her peripheral vision, and on instinct, she grabbed it. She pulled it forward and plunged the glowing blade into his chest.

More power surged into her body. Something new. It combined with the forces already inside of her, and a flash of light burst before her eyes.

Catriona fell from her perch on Huck. He was gone. No pile of ash—just *gone*. Anne sat on her butt several feet away from her as if an explosion had blown her there.

Catriona took a deep breath to steady her ragged heartbeat.

"What happened?" she asked.

"You siphoned him by yourself," said Anne, getting to her feet. "You took my sword and—" The pirate seemed at a loss for words. "I think you took a piece of it."

She held up a hand, and her orange sword flickered to life.

"But you still have it," said Catriona.

"Most of it." Anne offered her a hand. "I know you've been through a lot, but we have to finish. Let's test a theory."

Catriona felt shell-shocked. She allowed Anne to lead her to an unconscious man laying where Con had left him, his jaw shifted at an unnatural angle.

Her body throbbed with power. It made her dizzy. She couldn't shake the feeling someone was watching her.

"Do it. Alone," said Anne.

Catriona lowered to her knees. She lay her hands on the man.

A moment later, he was gone.

Anne gaped. "You're self-sufficient now."

Catriona looked around at the few standing bodies remaining—a befuddled handful of Kairos whose repeated attempts to escape the area had been thwarted by the Angeli transportation service.

One of them was Rune. He skulked near the giant rock, muttering to himself, trying to inch away unnoticed.

Anne clenched her fists, readying her sword. "We need to—"

Catriona put a hand on the pirate's arm.

"There's an easier way."

Looking at the remaining crowd, she'd finally identified the odd sensation haunting her since she finished Huck.

She felt them *all*.

She sensed all the corrupted Kairos—not just the ones remaining in the desert amphitheater, but everywhere—scattered around the world. Glowing threads connected them all, each body a point of light. She could see the web in her mind's eye.

She was one of those points.

She saw it as plainly as the desert around her.

"Step back," she said.

She concentrated, imagining herself moving along those glistening threads like morning dew gliding across a spider web. When she reached a corrupted point of light, it flickered and disappeared. As she absorbed them, she grew faster, *stronger*.

Behind her, the lights flickered back to life again, bright and uncorrupted.

"*Stop*."

Rune's voice echoed in her head.

She paused her travels.

"*Stop*," he said again.

Catriona knew *this* was why Rune had been absorbing his acolytes. He'd been desperately trying to absorb enough power to access the web—but the crowd had run from him. He wasn't fast enough to catch them. He didn't have angels delivering bodies to him.

Rune had opened the door enough to peek at the web on which she traveled, but he lacked the power to affect it.

"I will not stop," said Catriona, pressing harder. More lights popped from sight.

Rune was bellowing now, powerless to stop her.

She clenched her fists as the last of the corrupted lights flickered from view.

Only Rune's remained.

"*Daughter.*"

His voice sounded different.

Catriona opened her eyes, her body pulsating with power.

Rune walked toward her with his hands outstretched. Anne stood nearby, her sword ready.

"Daughter," he repeated.

She watched his approach.

"You see me *now*?" she asked.

He smiled. "Of course. I've always seen you."

Catriona smiled back at him.

Lies.

She closed her eyes and located that last remaining corrupted point of light on the glowing web.

"*Poof*," she said.

She opened her eyes in time to see the flash as Rune disappeared.

Catriona dropped to the dust. With Rune's passing, it felt as if all the energy she'd been collecting had dissipated.

The web disappeared.

She was herself again.

She was alone again.

CHAPTER FORTY-THREE

One month later.

"Sean said I might find you here," said Pete, sitting on the bench beside Catriona.

She smiled.

He followed her focus to where it was pointed.

"You know that's a fake grave, right?"

She nodded. She'd been coming to the Parasol Pictures set of an Irish mystery, much of which took place in a graveyard. It wasn't Scotland, and it wasn't Broch, but she'd found it comforting to sit on the bench there and talk to the gravestone of the fallen warrior from the movie.

A little part of her had hoped she'd wake up to find Broch back at home one day. Gog had divined how to teleport himself right into her apartment. Surely, the man who swore he lived to love her could too?

Gog, for crying out loud.

But after the battle in Joshua Tree, there'd been no sign of Broch. She imagined he was a baby somewhere, maybe decades or centuries away, swaddled in plaid.

Sean had planned to tell the studio his son had died unexpectedly, but she'd refused to let him. She told him to tell everyone he'd left. She'd rather have the world think she'd failed another relationship than admit Broch was dead.

"Fiona said you took the breakup pretty hard," said Pete. "I've been worried about you. I haven't seen you around."

She shrugged. "I'm fine. Did you need something?"

He nodded. "Sean said they've got a report of a disturbance at the gate. He said your phone was turned off."

She glanced at her phone. She'd silenced it.

She sighed. "I'm on it."

Pete stood. "You know, if you, you know, ever want to grab some food—as friends, not a date—I'm here for you."

She took his hand, and he helped her up. "Thanks, Pete. I might take you up on that."

The moment she stood, he threw his arms around her. He squeezed her, and she let him.

"That was a stunning display of emotion for you," she said when he'd finished.

He grimaced. "I hope *I* didn't have anything to do with you guys breaking up? I mean, the way I was trying to sabotage—"

She snorted a laugh. "It wasn't you."

The memory of Pete trying to steal Broch's ring made her look at the band on her finger.

Pete scowled. "I don't think it's healthy to keep wearing that."

She shrugged. "I'll take it off soon."

They walked together to their respective golf carts parked outside the soundstage.

"Thanks, Pete. I'll give you a call," she said.

He nodded and wheeled off.

She drove to the front gate to find the guard there scrolling through his phone.

"You've got a nuisance?" she asked.

He looked up, saw it was her, and quickly put down the phone. "Oh. Yeah. It's this guy. I wasn't sure how we should handle it when someone keeps coming back."

"Do you think he's dangerous?"

He shook his head. "I don't know. He seems more confused than angry."

"Is he still here?"

He looked outside his guard box. "He went that way today. He usually goes the other way."

Catriona nodded. She'd go take a peek. She had nothing better to do. "I'll have a look. Try and give me a call first thing next time."

"Will do."

Catriona left her golf cart and walked down the sidewalk beside the large stone wall surrounding the studio. Rounding a corner, she spotted a body clinging to the stone wall, dangling ten feet in the air.

"Hey," she called. "Get down off of there."

The man froze, hiding in the vines.

She waited for him to move, but he didn't.

She couldn't help but chuckle.

"I can still see you when you're not moving, buddy. You're not a rabbit, and I'm not a fox. Get down."

The guy started back down the wall until he was low enough to drop to the ground. Catriona took a step back to give herself extra reaction time. Who knew if the weirdo would take a swipe at her? He was *big*. One smack might send her flying.

The man landed and straightened to his full, impressive height. He turned to face her.

Catriona gasped.

"*Kilty*," she said.

His brow knit. He didn't seem to recognize her.

"Eh?"

She swallowed.

"Why are you trying to get on the lot?" she asked.

He ran his hand over his buzzcut head.

"Ah dinnae ken. Ah just ken ah need tae be in *there*. There's somethin'..." He squinted at her. "Dae ah ken ye?"

She didn't know what to say. Should she tell him everything? *Now?* Risk frightening him away?

"Um, would you like a tour?" she said instead.

He seemed pleased by the idea. "Aye. That would be *fine*."

She nodded and headed back toward the entrance. "Follow me."

He jogged to catch up and walk beside her. "Aye, ah came all the way fae Scootland tae see this place, and ah'm nae sure howfur."

"You're *kidding*," she said, smirking. "You're from Scotland? I *never* would have guessed."

"Aye." He looked at her and blushed. "Ah dinnae regret it, though. Comin' here. Not noo."

Catriona glanced at him and then looked away. She felt trapped somewhere between giddy excitement and tears.

It was Broch, wasn't it? It was, obviously, to look at him— but would he ever be *her* Broch again?

"What's your name?" she asked.

He paused for too long.

"You're not sure?" she teased.

He flashed a sheepish smile. "Brochan. *Broch*."

Her attention snapped to him.

Same name. That's a good sign, isn't it?

"Any chance you need a job?" she asked. "Maybe a place to stay?"

Broch's expression broadened with what looked like delighted surprise.

"Ah *dae*. Howfur did ye ken?"

She shrugged. "Oh, just a guess."

They walked on. Broch's strides grew shorter and slower as they passed through the studio gates until he stopped.

Catriona paused to look at him.

"Are you okay?"

He blinked at her. She couldn't read the strange expression on his face. He looked frightened.

"Broch?"

Broch's eyes grew glassy. He reached out to her, looking wobbly. Catriona reached out to grip his upturned wrist.

"Are you okay?" she repeated. Something seemed very wrong. The sight of him looking so sad and scared broke her heart.

His gaze dropped to her fingers resting on his arm. He took her hand and ran his thumb over her engagement ring.

His eyes met hers again.

"Catriona?" he whispered.

Catriona gasped at the sound of her name on his lips. A tightness built behind her eyes.

"Yes?"

His expression cracked and he threw his arms around her.

"Catriona— *mo ghràdh, mo cuishle*."

He kissed her face until exhausted by tears, and she buried her face in his chest. To feel him against her again, to have him back—her heart threatened to burst.

"You remember me?" she asked.

He leaned back to hold her at arm's length.

"Ah remember *everythin'*."

She smiled as his brow furrowed.

"What's wrong?" she asked.

His head cocked. "Dae ye still hae mah kilt?"

She laughed.

"I *do*. It's been waiting for you, Kilty."

She took his hand.
"Let's go home," she said.
He nodded.
"Aye."

~~ **THE END** ~~

WANT SOME MORE? FREE PREVIEWS!

If you liked this book, read on for a preview of the next Kilty AND the Shee McQueen Mystery-Thriller Series!

THANK YOU FOR READING!

If you enjoyed this book, please swing back to Amazon and **leave me a review** — even short reviews help authors like me find new fans! You can also FOLLOW AMY on AMAZON

ABOUT THE AUTHOR

USA Today and Wall Street Journal bestselling author Amy Vansant has written over 20 books, including the fun, thrilling Shee McQueen series, the rollicking, twisty Pineapple Port Mysteries, and the action-packed Kilty urban fantasies. Throw in a couple romances and a YA fantasy for her nieces...

Amy specializes in fun, exciting reads with plenty of laughs and action -- she tried to write serious books, but they always ended up full of jokes, so she gave up.

Amy lives in Jupiter, Florida with her muse/husband and a goony Bordoodle named Archer.

Books by Amy Vansant

Pineapple Port Mysteries
Funny, clean & full of unforgettable characters

Shee McQueen Mystery-Thrillers
Action-packed, fun romantic mystery-thrillers

Kilty Urban Fantasy/Romantic Suspense
Action-packed romantic suspense/urban fantasy

Slightly Romantic Comedies
Classic romantic romps

The Magicatory
Middle-grade fantasy

FREE PREVIEW

KILTY HISTORY

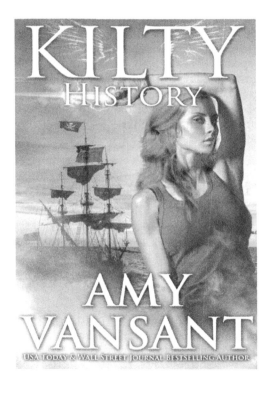

CHAPTER ONE

Sea Isle City, New Jersey

Anne Bonny sat at a small metal table at an outdoor café in Sea Isle City, New Jersey, staring dreamily at the mimosa tree arching above her table. The tree's fuzzy pink flowers gave her the impression of a Dr. Seuss creation as if Horton himself had decorated it for a summer holiday.

The rhythmic crashing of the surf, a soothing *whoosh*, served as the soundtrack to her peaceful day. Around the restaurant's wrought iron table tiny sparrows hopped across the eating area, snatching spare crumbs like little feathered vacuum cleaners. A block away, a seagull cackled its wild, agitated laugh.

With only a young couple in love cooing to each other nearby, Anne enjoyed her hard-earned tranquility. She'd decided to steal a few days away from her apartment in New York City to explore the New Jersey, Delaware, and Maryland shores and doodled on a folded map as she pondered her route. Should she pause in Cape May? Take the ferry to Delaware?

More importantly, now that the last bit of French toast had disappeared from her plate, where would she have lunch?

The female half of the cooing couple stood, scraping her metal chair across the stone pavers. Anne watched the girl in the form-fitting tank dress twitch her way into the main building. Anne made brief eye contact with the young man still at the table, flashed him a polite *whoops, we made eye-contact* smile and returned to her thoughts.

Anne reached for an overlooked crumb of bacon on her plate as the sparrows flew away in unison. Savoring the last of Bacon Heaven, her sharp gaze swept the area to find the cause of their unrest.

"Great little arse," said a man's voice in an Irish accent.

Anne sat upright and trained her gaze back on her patio

neighbor. The sandy-haired young man, still sitting where his girl had left him, met Anne's curious gaze with a wicked grin. He stood and dragged his chair to her table with a teeth-rattling screech of metal on stone.

The boy released an overly dramatic sigh, plopped into the chair positioned beside Anne, and beckoned the server as she exited the café and stepped out onto the patio.

"Could I get four whiskeys here?" he asked, dangling his finger over the table and swirling it as if mixing a drink.

The server smirked. "Uh, sure...what kind?"

The boy's gaze swiveled to Anne.

"Something Irish and as expensive as possible," he said putting his right elbow on the table and resting his head on it. He stared as he spoke to the server, his attention never leaving Anne. "*Straight*. You can put it on her tab. Or mine. Doesn't matter really. I'm not paying either way."

Anne sighed. "*His* tab."

The waitress ogled Anne, no doubt wondering what the young man's girlfriend would think of his new friend, and then left to fetch the whiskey.

"Ooh, Annie, I love that evil streak of yours. You're going to stick the lad with my tab."

Anne's new table guest sat grinning, thin and pale as an untoasted wafer, but with the fiery eyes of a rebellious imp eager to be unleashed. She'd known the minute she heard the Irish accent the boy wasn't *the boy* anymore. Con Carey, her longtime friend, and lover, who'd lost his corporeal body some years ago in a work-related accident, had *appropriated* the boy's body. Like a wicked spirit, since losing his flesh, Con borrowed other people's to communicate.

Unlike a ghost, the only thing scary about Con was his otherworldly ability to consume whiskey.

"Hello, Con. Did you ask that poor boy if you could borrow his body?"

"Hello, my love. Absolutely not. They almost always say no."

Anne recalled how thrilled Con had been the first time he'd found a way to use another person's body. He'd pumped his fists and run around the room screaming with joy until he crashed over a sofa, having lost control of his borrowed legs.

"How are you, lass? Did you miss me?"

Before she could answer, Con leaped to his feet and did

jumping jacks. Wrapped in the young man's bony frame, he boxed an invisible opponent for a few moments, and then clapped himself on either shoulder, pleased with his performance.

"Featherweight," he said, flopping back into his chair.

"Feather*brain*." Anne paused as the server returned to set four whiskeys on the table. Unsure how to dole the shots, she lumped them in the middle of the table.

Con took the first and swallowed it before the waitress released the last glass from her grasp.

Anne arched an eyebrow. "Slow down. She could have lost a finger."

"Uhhhhmmmm..." Con ignored Anne in his ecstasy.

She watched with amusement as Con licked his lips. As a disembodied spirit, Con's lack of lips made it difficult for him to enjoy the finer things in life. She could see he was in heaven.

Anne snatched the second whiskey from the table, shot it back, and slapped the empty glass into Con's hand. He jerked his paw from the empty shot glass as if it burned his fingertips. Jaw clenched, he clamped his fingers around the next full shot, training his eyes on Anne's, daring her to touch it.

He raised the third shot to his mouth.

Anne grinned. *Not a chance.*

With inhuman speed, she snatched the glass from Con's fingers and pressed it against her bottom lip, threatening to drink.

"Harpy!" Con roared, slamming his fist to the table. The glasses jumped on the wrought iron.

Anne paused, allowing the drama to grow, and then returned the glass with a bow of her head. Visibly relieved, Con downed the shot and wiped his mouth on the back of his hand.

"Surely, ye know better than to break me heart like that. Ye might have spilled it."

Anne grinned, incapable of staying annoyed with Con for long. She *was* happy to see him, even if he inhabited the body of yet another innocent passerby. He hadn't made one of his appearances in months.

She wasn't sure what to do when the girl returned from the ladies' room expecting to find her boyfriend waiting for her and not chatting up the busty strawberry blonde at the next table. She hadn't been in a catfight in ages.

"I wish you would time these visits better. His girlfriend will be here any second."

"I'll be quick."

Anne nodded and took small solace in the fact that Con had chosen a *boy* to borrow. During a past impromptu visit, Con had possessed the body of a young woman and given Anne a sloppy kiss in front of the girl's grandmother. The poor girl was probably still trying to explain that.

Anne nodded to the empty whiskey glasses. "You know what they say, drinky, drinky, little dinky," she held up her pinky and waggled it for effect.

Con gaped in mock horror, the last shot nearly to his lips. He put down the glass, pulled out the waistband of his plaid shorts, and peered inside. With a shrug, he snapped them shut.

"Sorry, Luv, but it looks as though I might as well drink."

Anne chuckled. "So why are you here?"

"I've come to give you a warning. Your pal is on the move."

"My pal?"

"Michael." Con turned his head to feign spitting on the floor in disgust as he said Michael's name. "There's trouble. I haven't been able to gather all the details yet, but something's afoot."

"Is that where you've been the last few months? Spying on Michael?"

Con raised one of the empty shot glasses, smelled it, and thrust his tongue inside to sop up the last drops.

"I said: *have you been spying on Michael?*" repeated Anne, taking the glass out of his hand and placing it back on the table.

Con pouted.

"Yes, I've been spying. Among other things."

Anne pretended Con's news meant nothing to her, but her chest felt tight. Seeming to sense her distress, Con placed his hand on hers. She smiled, realizing what a poor actress she was.

"Ye'll be fine, ye always are. I just wanted ye to prepare yourself."

Without warning, Con leaned forward and put his hand on the back of Anne's head, pulling her face to his. He ravished her with a kiss.

Anne marveled how strange it was the kiss felt like *Con* and not like the stranger whose lips *actually* pressed against her own.

The smell of whiskey helped.

She gave into the kiss. As she did, Con left his host and Anne found herself lip-locked with a very confused young man.

"What are you *doing*?" came a screech from across the patio.

Anne's eyes popped wide, her lips still pressed against the young man's. His girlfriend had returned and now stood, jaw slack, pointing at Anne.

The boy jerked back from Anne's kiss, holding his arms wide as if declaring himself safe on base.

"Wha...?" He stood and put his fingers on the table to steady himself as the full effect of three whiskies and a recent possession took their toll on what Anne guessed to be a hundred thirty-five pound frame.

He stared at his girlfriend, jaw working but no words coming. When he turned back to Anne, his gaze fell on her cleavage and she watched him try to squelch a grin. He burped and raised his hand to his mouth.

"Why do I taste booze?" he asked no one in particular.

"*What are you doing*?" the girl's tone reached a glass-breaking screech level.

"He agreed to test our new line of lipsticks." Anne stood and gathered her things before moving toward the restaurant's back door. "He earned *you* a free sampler kit from us, which I'll go get from the car now."

The girl's pinched glower relaxed a notch as she seemed to find herself torn between free makeup and an implausible explanation for her boyfriend's roving lips. She took a step toward her equally confused boyfriend and sniffed.

"Why *do* you smell like booze?"

"*Whiskey*-flavored lipstick," Anne called over her shoulder as she entered the restaurant. "*Irish Rose*."

Anne paid her tab and the young couple's at the register and left the café.

On the street, Anne considered Con's message. Any time Con noticed Michael acting suspiciously, bad things followed.

Michael was an Angelus, a member of a race of creatures whose sole duty was to ensure the safety of the human race. Anne was a Sentinel. She worked for the Angeli as a sort of bounty hunter, helping to track and kill Perfidia—Angeli who preyed on humans instead of protecting them. Whenever

Michael called her, she knew a battle lay ahead, and while she'd once relished such challenges, her enthusiasm had waned. A Perfidian had nearly killed Con. Since then, Anne had felt death was her constant companion.

It didn't help that she and Michael were involved in a complicated romance, which added stress to every exchange.

Anne wished she could fly away from the whole mess, but today, disappearing would be especially difficult. As she scanned the street outside the café, she found her parking spot occupied by a new tenant.

Her Jaguar had gone A.W.O.L.

"Blast." Anne strode from one end of the block to the other, searching for her car. Peering between two beachside duplexes, she finally spotted it parked on the next block.

I know I didn't park there.

Anne scowled. Maybe Con had moved the car as a joke before he visited her at the café? That fit his M.O. Or, maybe she was going senile. She *was* slightly over three hundred years old. A long life was one of the benefits of working for Angeli—assuming she could stay alive with Perfidia constantly trying to kill her.

Anne cut between the beach houses toward her vehicle, ducking and slipping through a small fence to enter a secluded backyard. Before she could stand upright, the figure of a man appeared in front of her.

Anne lacked even a second to react.

The man raised a small pistol and shot her directly between the eyes.

CHAPTER TWO

Jamaica, 1720

"I can't believe I just stole a ship," said Anne, staring out across the Caribbean Sea as Captain Rackham wrapped his wiry arms around her waist.

He murmured in her ear. "You're a pirate now."

She grinned.

I'm a pirate now.

She felt far away from Charles Town, South Carolina, where she'd grown up after her father, William Cormac, fled Ireland to escape the shame of his affair with Anne's mother, Mary Brennan. Mary had been his maidservant, and the good Catholics of County Cork didn't approve of his behavior.

Anne hadn't been born to be a pirate, but there was no denying *naughty* ran in her blood.

Blessed with her mother's milky complexion and copper tresses, Anne had suffered no shortage of attention from boys during her time in Charles Town. At seventeen, she'd met James Bonny, who'd hoped to win her father's fortune by marrying into the family. James was a rascal, a sailor, and a small-time pirate. Anne could never decide if James was truly *handsome*, but he drove her father mad, and that was enough.

James' visits to her home always coincided with the disappearance of household items. When her frustrated father made it clear she had to choose between her inattentive family and her thieving boyfriend, Anne gathered everything she could carry and eloped with James to Nassau, Bahamas.

Just a few months later, in the summer of 1718, English Governor Woodes Rogers came to Nassau and James Bonny ended his fledgling pirate career to become an informant for Woodes, *ratting* on the very scoundrels he once claimed as bosom pals. Snug in the pocket of the new Governor, Anne's husband increasingly ignored her in favor of his glamorous new friends.

Anne found herself spending her copious idle time at the local pub with the charming Captain John "Calico Jack" Rackham, a *real* pirate who called Nassau his homeport. Rackham had a kinder face, quicker wit, and easier humor than James. More importantly, he promised to whisk Anne away from her tedious life in Nassau.

When the opportunity arose, Rackham, Anne, a stolen sloop called *The Revenge*, and a makeshift crew of rascals escaped Nassau and sailed miles away before dawn the following day.

The Revenge sat three days from a much-needed stop in Jamaica when Blue, the afternoon lookout man, spotted something off the port bow.

"There's a woman in the sea," he mumbled to Anne when she approached to investigate.

She sighed.

Blue's been in the whiskey again.

Snatching his spyglass, she peered across the sea to spot a small boat. Indeed, there was a female figure inside, lost or cast adrift.

Poor thing. Probably dead.

Rackham took his turn with the spyglass and ordered his crew to investigate. Half an hour of rowing later, they returned with a woman wearing tattered brown robes.

From the moment the stranger arrived on *The Revenge*, Anne couldn't peel her gaze from her. The castaway's features were foreign. Her brow was heavy; her eyes slanted like those of an exotic Anne had met once in St. Croix. On boarding, the woman had smiled at Anne, displaying fine white teeth that belied an easier life than Anne would have guessed for her, judging from the woman's ratty clothing. As quickly as her brilliant grin appeared, it was gone, and the woman resumed her solemn, almost regal demeanor as the men led her onto the ship.

Anne marveled as the usually rowdy crew gave the strange woman a wide berth. They seemed frightened of her. She offered their guest water and food, but for someone plucked from the sea, she was strangely uninterested in both. She refused to speak. Often, Anne caught the woman's gaze on her.

"Why do you stare at me?" she asked finally, unnerved.

The woman smiled and pointed at the sea.

A frigate had appeared from nowhere. No sooner did Anne spot the ship, than the warning call came from the lookouts and the boat lurched beneath her feet.

The Revenge was under attack.

She grabbed the stranger's arm and pointed to the hold. "Hide."

The woman kept her feet planted on the deck and smiled.

Shortly after the initial attack, Jonathan Barnet, the man charged with ridding the local waters of pirates by the Governor of Jamaica, forcibly boarded *The Revenge* with his men.

Anne had no idea what to do. There was no handbook for fledgling pirates, or if there was, Captain Jack hadn't shared it with her.

Does this sort of thing happen all the time? Maybe Rackham just needs to pay him and he'll go away?

She watched in horror as one of Barnet's men stabbed one of her fellow pirates straight through.

Or not.

She glanced at the strange woman, who was now squatting on the deck beside her and had an idea. The attacking ship was crewed by British soldiers. There was no reason for anyone to think that Anne herself wasn't a captive. After all, she'd only been a pirate for a little over a day...

Anne grasped the woman's arm and tried to pull her to her feet. She needed to take her to safety in the belly of the ship, where the two of them could pretend they'd been kidnapped.

She tugged, but the woman felt as though she weighed as much as the ship itself.

"Come on! You're going to die here!"

The castaway refused to budge.

Anne felt a shadow fall across them. Pulling her blade from her side, she whirled to thrust at her attacker. The man yelped and fell back.

Anne found her knife covered in blood. Crimson oozed across her white-knuckled grip on the hilt.

Stunned by the sight of death on her weapon, she never sensed the second soldier approaching.

His sword plunged deep into her lower abdomen.

Anne clutched her stomach and fell to her knees, her knife clattering to the deck. She slumped, following it to the ground.

The sounds of battle receded as she struggled to breathe, pain burning in her side. Her eyes fluttered shut. When she opened them again, she found the pearly-toothed grin of the strange woman inches from her face.

Anne lay on her back, her head bent awkwardly against the wall of the upper deck, powerless to move as the woman began whispering in a foreign language.

The woman's breath smelled like cinnamon and ginger.

When Anne next awoke, it was daylight. Her arms felt bound to her sides. A scratchy fabric covered her face. Her legs, too, were immovable.

Anne took a deep breath and tried to find her voice.

"Help," she croaked, her throat dry.

Anne heard a collective gasp. Men began to chatter.

Rackham's voice boomed. "Don't just stand there; help her!"

Hands fell on her, scrambling to rip the covering from her face. She felt a rush of relief as her bindings gave way and she could once again move her arms and legs.

Freed, Anne sat bolt upright. She was on the deck of *The Revenge*, surrounded by what remained of the crew. On either side of her lay a dozen human shapes wrapped in burlap. They were very, very still.

Anne scrambled away from the bodies.

"Anne!"

Mary Read, a tavern server who'd followed Anne to *The Revenge*, burst from the crowd to embrace her. Anne hugged her back, still reeling with confusion.

"You're alive." Captain Rackham moved toward her. "My God, girl, how?"

Anne punched the Captain in the chest with the underside of her fist.

"You were going to throw me into the sea?"

Rackham plucked at Anne's middle, the fabric of her shirt torn and stained reddish-brown. Anne rolled back the cloth to reveal her smooth, unmarked belly. She recalled the pain of the soldier's sword piercing her flesh and searched for the wound.

She found nothing.

"You were a goner, I swear," said Rackham.

Anne scanned her shipmates. The grungy crew stood silently, eying her, their expressions chock with suspicion.

Rising from the dead would gain her no friends among the superstitious crew.

"It must be someone else's blood? I am unharmed. You should have checked more carefully." She forced a giggle. Surely, demons didn't giggle. The crew had to know that.

Calico Jack Rackham gripped Anne's shoulders and looked into her eyes. It felt as though he was trying to read her mind. She didn't flinch, hiding her fear with a mask of simple joy.

"You should lie down," Rackham said, pulling her toward his cabin.

Anne heard the splash of the corpses hitting the sea behind her as she followed Rackham. She turned and saw the crew give each body a good poking before pushing it overboard, just to be sure.

In his cabin, Rackham had Anne disrobe. He inspected every inch of her flesh for injuries. She could only shrug and smile at his confusion. It was becoming easier to smile.

Physically, she felt *amazing*.

"What happened to the woman we pulled from the sea?" she asked.

He waved a hand dismissively. "Gone. Missing."

Anne tried to recall what the woman had whispered to her,

but only remembered one line.

Find the angel.

She assumed the woman had been praying for her.

Captain Rackham admitted defeat in his search for Anne's wounds. He kissed her and pulled her hips against his own. Pressing his face against her neck, he inhaled.

"You smell fantastic. Like cinnamon..."

Anne pushed Rackham back to look him in the eye.

"And ginger?"

"Yes." He nodded. "Now that you mention it; cinnamon and ginger."

GET *KILTY HISTORY* ON AMAZON!

ANOTHER FREE PREVIEW!

THE GIRL WHO WANTS

A Shee McQueen Mystery-Thriller by Amy Vansant

Chapter One

Three Weeks Ago, Nashua, New Hampshire.

Shee realized her mistake the moment her feet left the grass.

He's enormous.

She'd watched him drop from the side window of the house. He landed four feet from where she stood, and still, her brain refused to register the warning signs. The nose, big and lumpy as breadfruit, the forehead some beach town could use as a jetty if they buried him to his neck...

His knees bent to absorb his weight and *her* brain thought, *got you.*

Her brain couldn't be bothered with simple math: *Giant, plus Shee, equals Pain.*

Instead, she jumped to tackle him, dangling airborne as his knees straightened and the *pet the rabbit* bastard stood to his full height.

Crap.

The math added up pretty quickly after that.

Hovering like Superman mid-flight, there wasn't much she could do to change her disastrous trajectory. She'd *felt* like a superhero when she left the ground. Now, she felt more like a Canada goose staring into the propellers of Captain Sully's Airbus A320.

She might take down the plane, but it was going to *hurt.*

Frankenjerk turned toward her at the same moment she plowed into him. She clamped her arms around his waist like a little girl hugging a redwood. Lurch returned the embrace, twisting her to the ground. Her back hit the dirt and air burst from her lungs like a double shotgun blast.

Ow.

Wheezing, she punched upward, striking Beardless Hagrid

in the throat.

That didn't go over well.

Grabbing her shoulder with one hand, Dickasaurus flipped her on her stomach like a sausage link, slipped his hand under her chin and pressed his forearm against her windpipe.

The only air she'd gulped before he cut her supply stank of damp armpit. He'd tucked her cranium in his arm crotch, much like the famous noggin-less horseman once held his severed head. Fireworks exploded in the dark behind her eyes.

That's when a thought occurred to her.

I haven't been home in fifteen years.

What if she died in Gigantor's armpit? Would her father even know?

Has it really been that long?

Flopping like a landed fish, she forced her assailant to adjust his hold and sucked a breath as she flipped on her back. Spittle glistened on his lips, his brow furrowed as if she'd asked him to read a paragraph of big-boy words.

His nostrils flared like the Holland Tunnel.

There's an idea.

Making a V with her fingers, Shee thrust upward, stabbing into his nose, straining to reach his tiny brain.

Goliath roared. Jerking back, he grabbed her arm to unplug her fingers from his nose socket. She whipped away her limb before he had a good grip, fearing he'd snap her bones with his Godzilla paws.

Kneeling before her, he clamped both hands over his face, cursing as blood seeped from behind his fingers.

Shee's gaze didn't linger on that mess. Her focus fell to his crotch, hovering a foot above her feet, protected by nothing but a thin pair of oversized sweatpants.

Scrambled eggs, sir?

She kicked.

He howled.

Shee scuttled back like a crab, found her feet, and snatched her gun from her side. The gun she should have pulled *before* trying to tackle the Empire State Building.

"Move a muscle and I'll aerate you," she said. She always liked that line.

The golem growled, but remained on the ground like a good dog, cradling his family jewels.

Shee's partner in this manhunt, a local cop easier on the eyes than he was useful, rounded the corner and drew his own weapon.

She smiled and holstered the gun he'd lent her. Unknowingly.

"Glad you could make it."

Her portion of the operation accomplished, she headed toward the car as more officers swarmed the scene.

"Shee, where are you going?" called the cop.

She stopped and turned.

"Home, I think."

His gaze dropped to her hip.

"Is that my gun?"

Get *The Girl Who Wants* on Amazon!

Vansant Creations, LLC / Amy Vansant
Jupiter, FL
http://www.AmyVansant.com

Proofreading by Effrosyni Moschoudi, Meg Barnhart
Cover by Lance Buckley & Amy Vansant

Made in United States
North Haven, CT
06 July 2024

54454086R30115